The Last Armenian

THE LAST ARMENIAN

by

Francis Rolt

HAMISH HAMILTON · LONDON

All the characters in this novel are people of the imagination; any similarity between them and real people, living or dead, is coincidental. Responsibility for the plot and opinions expressed rests entirely with the author and should not be blamed on any friends he may have in Bangladesh or elsewhere.

Excerpt from "Trial By Fire" reprinted by permission from TIME. Copyright 1963 Time Inc. All rights reserved.

First published in Great Britain 1987
by Hamish Hamilton Ltd
27 Wrights Lane London W8 5TZ
All rights reserved
Copyright © 1987 by Francis Rolt

British Library Cataloguing in Publication Data
Rolt, Francis
The last Armenian.
I. Title
823'.914[F]   PR6068.04/
ISBN 0-241-12344-5

Typeset in $11\frac{1}{2}/12\frac{1}{2}$pt Sabon by Butler & Tanner Ltd
Printed and bound in Great Britain
by Butler & Tanner Ltd, Frome, Somerset

To John and Rachel, Mary, Peter and Mark.

'When you do not realise that you are one with the universe, you have fear. Whether it is separated into drops or not, water is water.'

Shrunryu Suzuki

'If one knows but does not act accordingly, one knows imperfectly.'

Marie-Jean Guyau

Part One

1

I COULD HARDLY have been further from Shiuli in mind or body, but a chance encounter brought her back, the memories overwhelming me like a storm.

I'd spent the afternoon in one of Kathmandu's second-hand bookshops searching through piles of dusty, yellowing paperbacks for anything of interest among the endless volumes by Castaneda, Gurdjieff and Krishnamurti. The shop smelt strongly of the *bidis* which the plump proprietor, reclining indolently on cushions at the rear of the shop, smoked incessantly.

From there I bicycled slowly through Durbar Square, Indra Chowk and Assan Tol, the labyrinthine lanes choked with colour and the substance of myths, past the King's Palace, out beyond the Newar villages which have been subsumed by the city itself, and down the straight road between terraced fields to Boddhnath Stupa. I pushed the bicycle around the great whitewashed mass of the Stupa, far below its all-seeing eyes, its eight golden steps to Enlightenment and the hundreds of prayer flags fluttering between its pinnacle and the periphery, their printed prayers fading in the sunlight, leaking their devotion into the clear winter sky.

I paid little attention to the usual eddying crowd: Tibetan shopkeepers, tall Sherpa women, Newars, Gurungs, Tamangs, pilgrims to the Stupa, and a scattering of tourists. My mind was taken up with mundane everyday thoughts. Then a metallic chink, slight in itself and hardly audible above the chatter and bustle, made me glance to the left where an Indian woman was watching people pass. She was young and attractive but not unusual or particularly striking. Still looking at her I walked on, unsettled by the familiar but, for an instant, unclassifiable sound. As I stared she pushed a series of silver bangles up one arm then let them fall back. They flashed like a spray of water drops at the bottom of a waterfall and tinkled as lightly as any distant yak bell across a high valley. The gesture and sound acted on my memory like a mnemonic.

Shiuli had had the same habit, the musical chink of silver on silver often mixing with her laugh, weighting its allure. Always that laugh, even after Jo's death she was able to summon it from the depths of her being and use it to challenge the gods, to demonstrate their powerlessness. The winter sun slanted into the marketplace and people brushed past me, but I ignored them, unable to counter the shock of being engulfed by Shiuli again; her voice, her face and her deep-throated laugh.

The Indian woman, suddenly aware of and embarrassed by my fixed gaze, turned away and involved herself in negotiations with a carpetseller.

Memories and images began to flow like a cyclone sweeping over the flat land from the Bay of Bengal, circling dangerously around the still centre. Shiuli's six bangles glittering on her dark arm. The light caught and held by the intricacy of the worked metal, giving the silver a life of its own. At times her wrist seemed to be encircled by living things which stroked and stayed close to her, luxuriating in the warmth her flesh afforded. I remember her dark, impassive face; an impassivity born of experience. One of her earliest memories, she once told me, was of a mother sweeping down on her and another girl on their first day in Primary School. The woman grabbed her daughter roughly by the arm and with the words, 'Come! Don't play with *dhabhor*,' dragged her away.

'What is *dhabhor*?' I had asked.

'Untouchables. Hindu sweepers imported from Madras by the British to clean Chittagong's drains and latrines. Probably the woman meant no particular harm, but because I'm dark-skinned I'm obviously not from good society. No Aryan blood in me, riff-raff you might say.'

'Are you *dhabhor*?'

Shiuli laughed. 'I asked Jo that once and he was furious. I was eleven or twelve at the time and tired of the teasing in school which my dark skin excited. I thought that if I could explain why I was darker than most of the other children then things would become easier.

'"You're a woman, a woman!" Jo shouted. "*Dhabhor-shabhor* means nothing."

'I must have looked frightened for he suddenly picked me up in his arms and kissed me.

'"*Dhabhor* are only people like you and me. It doesn't matter where you came from. Such definitions are for those who want to limit their lives, border them with restrictions. The *dhabhor* are poor but at least they know they're alive, if only for a short time. That's the only true difference. If the others tease you for being dark you can say that their light skins prove them to be the descendants of pirates, Christians and Mughal land-grabbbers."

'I never tried, it sounded a little too insulting.

'No, I don't think I'm *dhabor*, just Bengali peasant. It's an intuitive feeling rather than anything else, but the races are so mixed up around here it doesn't make any difference.'

The remembrance of her defiant eyes then and at other times stabbed through the calm I had cultivated after that last terrible week in Chittagong, when my love for Shiuli and fear of what we'd become involved in warred with each other.

Men often misunderstood her direct gaze as a challenge and therefore an invitation. 'They think of me as a whore because they guess I'm sleeping with you and because I'm not afraid of them,' she explained after Nazmah's ex-husband had offered her money to sleep with her. 'Because I don't fit into any of their categories they believe that I have no rights, no rules and no morals. They don't understand a thing.'

She'd laughed in his face and called him an old pig. In Moslem Chittagong the insult had quietened a roomful of people, stunning them with its enormity. She'd left the party, the only sound her uneven step and the swish of her silk sari, as dry as the noise a swallow makes in flight. An hour later I found her weeping with hurt and anger in Shomela's room. Jo's old retainer was delighted by the insult.

'Old pig! Yes, yes he is,' Shomela laughed, wiping the tears from her eyes with a corner of sari. 'How can a man become so rich in a country like Bangladesh without stealing from everyone else? Old pig!'

My mind tried to impose some order on the confusing jumble of images which tore through me as I stood in the paved ring around the Stupa.

Boddhipal Bhikkhu's shaven head and honey-gold skin, drawn tightly over the delicate facial bones, formed itself and was instantly replaced in my mind's eye by Jo's moulded features fixed in rigid immobility. The stench of formaldehyde and corpses again stuffed my nostrils, but as though to lessen the horror of that image I seemed to hear Boddhipal saying:

'What you know as reality, this life, is a film of petrol over an ocean. Its pretty colours and changing patterns attract us, but if we light a match and fling it onto the petrol that insubstantial, meretricious beauty will disappear in a flash and a moment.'

In my imagination he sounded as though he were trying to convince himself as much as comfort me.

I saw Nazmah's hawk-like face too, animated in conversation, her thin hands sketching ideograms in the sunlight to give force to a statement. It was from her that I learnt something of the city's confused past; of how Buddhism was established under the third-century emperor Asoka, of the pilgrims who came from China and Tibet and who wrote about Chittagong's great Buddhist monastery—Pandita Vihara. It was she who told me that when Arab merchants captured the eastern spice trade in the ninth century they colonised the city and then lost it to the kingdom of Arakan. In 1338 it was annexed by the armour-bearer Fakhruddin Shah, who established Bengal's independence from the Delhi Sultans for two centuries under a succession of Persian, Afghan and Habshi slave dynasties. In the time of the Mughal emperor Shah Jehan the city was overrun by a Portuguese pirate, Bastion Gonzales, who took the king of Arakan's daughter in marriage and whose renegade followers from Goa, Sri Lanka, Cochin and Malacca pillaged and depopulated lower Bengal. It was Nazmah who told me that in 1666 the governor of Bengal, Shaista Khan, tricked the pirates into leaving the city, annexed it for the last great Mughal emperor, Aurangezeb, and denied them the means to return. I learnt of the creeping influence exercised by the East India Company, of the tyrannical indigo planters who tortured and murdered as they saw fit, and of the city's short-lived freedom from the British when the Armoury was captured by nationalists in 1930.

Out of this intractable knot of history had been born Shiuli. For me she was Chittagong's eye, around which all else revolved. Its packed streets loud with rickshaw bells, the shouts of fruit sellers, itinerant knife-grinders and quacks with magic potions for every ill, real or imagined. She was at the centre of its low conical hills rising abruptly out of the coastal plain, of its port and brothels, its gold market and the Club.

How mistaken the attempt to escape was. Peace means an unstringing of the need to remember which returns us unhesitatingly, bead by bead, to people and events which are close to our hearts; but it's not possible to sever the string itself. I realised that I couldn't even begin to unstring my need for Shiuli. In coming to Kathmandu I was trying to escape the city and events which seemed ready to devour me like some monstrous beast from Tibetan mythology. I tried to follow Boddhipal's example, to regard the world as an abstraction, its beauty and pain as toys to be dropped along the way.

When I first arrived in Kathmandu I told Lama Govinda that I was addicted to those abstractions as I might be addicted to opium dreams, knowing them to be dreams. But I'd wanted to blot out the past, not sever the string or overcome it.

Someone bumped into me and I began to walk home automatically. In the late afternoon light the Stupa's bulk glowed pale orange, while its symbolic golden steps reflected the setting sun with a fiery intensity. Two old Newar women tottered painfully around it, their hands pressed to their bent backs. They stopped before each of the dozens of prayer wheels set in the stone base and pushed feebly. A young Tibetan monk, absently telling beads with one hand, overtook them and strode ahead spinning each wheel vigorously as though to ensure that its prayers were flung far off the earth and into the Aether.

In the Stupa's shadow I pulled the Kashmir shawl more closely around my shoulders and hurried past the three beggars preparing to leave their accustomed position. Shivering in the cold air, I entered the alley where I rented two rooms, all I could afford on the little private tutoring I did. The sky was still a pale blue tinged here and there gold and red, but the alley was in deep shadow. The swallows which had been riding the wild air all day, screeching with excitement, were back in their nests. The old houses on either side towered up four storeys, their doors and shutters already closed tightly against *bhut*, the spirits which come out at night.

I pushed open the low wooden door, nearly four inches thick. Inside it was dark and my landlord's cow munched noisily, unaffected by the intrusion. At the top of the first flight of stairs I patted the wall cautiously for the broken light switch and continued up into the near-empty room adjoining my bedroom. All these actions were performed automatically, without thought, but still I sighed with relief as I closed the heavy trapdoor behind me, as though the task of returning had been both difficult and dangerous.

The stair light threw my shadow around the walls and beamed roof as I pulled up the shutter of one window, locking it open with a crude wooden latch. Cold air poured in. Sitting on the smooth mud floor I stared out across the empty terraces towards the mountains, their snow-capped peaks glowing pink. A solitary fruit bat, like some primeval harbinger of doom, flapped sluggishly south, making for its night-time feast. At dawn it would return to hang with hundreds of others in one of the tall eucalyptus trees on the rim of the Kathmandu Valley, to sleep off the night's excesses in the warmth of the sun.

2

MY THOUGHTS RETURN to the nightmare which grew like some fungus rotting the soft interior of my life, its thread-like roots liquefying and absorbing my will, leaving a dry shell. Within a week the spread of these insidious capillaries frightened me into abandoning Shiuli and drove me nearly a thousand kilometres, from Chittagong to Kathmandu.

Sravan: the month of coups and counter-coups, when tempers grow short under the double torture of an implacable humidity and a haze of dust blown up from the roads and fields surrounding the city. The month in which everyone waits for the monsoon to begin. Traders hoard rice and pray that it will break late, or not at all. The government watches the price of rice rising in the markets, threatens speculators and then sinks back into lethargy, overcome by the effort. Aid workers prepare for another possible disaster, study their statistics and recall the last famine; people dying, dead on the streets every day. Farmers look at the sky, watch their seedlings shrivel and borrow more at ruinous interest rates to try again.

I was in a rickshaw when it finally broke.

I peered out, past the rickshaw driver pedalling hard against the force of the wind and the warm, driving rain. We were the only moving object on the road, apart from leaves and rubbish borne along by the yellowish streams of water already three or four inches deep. The air was cool again after weeks of overwhelming humidity. I almost felt able to break the news of Jo's death to Shiuli. I imagined her sitting on our veranda watching the longed-for rain pouring off the roof and the thin palm trees while crows squawked and cursed, jumping from branch to branch and flapping their wings like so many old women in *burkhas*, black from head to toe, gossiping at the sight of a girl in Western clothes.

I'd been fending off the thought of telling her as I returned from the Cantonment, deliberately allowing the afternoon's heat to fur my mind, but the rain swept it clear again.

The rickshaw swerved to avoid an open storm drain, throwing me hard against the side of the gawdy hood. 'Go slowly,' I shouted, but the driver took no notice and I recognised my own indifference. To shout was my prerogative, to ignore me his. I watched his thin legs pumping up and down, the stringy sinews standing out as he drove the machine up the slight gradient of Jubilee Road.

I'd been marking exam scripts at home, sweat smudging the confused scrawls and making the task doubly difficult, when an army jeep pulled into the compound. An officer jumped out and came towards the house. Normally we had no dealings with the army and I met him on the veranda with some apprehension. He introduced himself as Major Rahman and in a few words told me that there was a corpse at the Cantonment which he believed to be that of Joseph Katchyan. He asked whether I would be able to give a positive identification. I stammered an affirmative reply, too shocked to be coherent.

We sat in the back of the jeep heading towards the Cantonment and he gave me the details.

'His car went over a ravine, a fifty-foot drop. You know what those roads are like at this time of year.'

I imagined it to be a rhetorical statement but there was a pause and he obviously expected me to respond.

'No, I don't. You know that foreigners aren't allowed beyond Kaptai or Rangamati.'

'Of course. So sorry, I was forgetting. Anyway it seems he braked, perhaps there was a monkey on the road, he could have mistaken it for a man in the headlights. The car skidded straight over. He was killed outright, the driving wheel stove in his chest. A patrol found him this morning. I'm afraid there's no doubt it's him but these formalities have to be gone through.'

Rahman had all the outward signs of command, including what I took to be a Sandhurst-trained voice; more at ease talking about a brace of pheasant than the accidental death of an elderly Armenian. His hands moved constantly, not with the definite movements I expected of a professional soldier, but more softly and slowly, as though pushing aside unseen obstacles.

'I see.' I couldn't think what else to say. Little things began to worry me. Had Jo made a will? Would he be difficult to recognise? What would we put on his gravestone? Such irrelevancies prevented me from having to think about Rahman's shattering information; with an effort I brushed them aside and asked where the accident had happened.

'Near Laxmichari in the Chengi Valley, the north end of the Hill Tracts. He had no right to be there anyway, not at night, not by himself. He might have been kidnapped or anything.' He sounded exasperated.

'"Anything" happened, didn't it? You're right.'

The major was embarrassed, he'd allowed his annoyance to show and was sensitive enough to realise that Jo had meant something to me. We finished the journey to the Cantonment, a few miles outside the city, in silence.

'You're a close friend of his daughter's aren't you?' The question was as blank as the neon-lit underground room, it hung in the air like the stench of chemicals, but seemed to imply more than that I lived in the same house. Although Shiuli and I had never hidden our attachment I was surprised that this army major should know of it. He seemed to feel sorry for me and continued, 'My wife knows a friend of yours quite well, they studied together at Dhaka University; Nazmah, Mushtaque Islam's daughter.' It was an explanation, almost an apology for his intrusive knowledge.

The body, I couldn't think of it as Jo, lay on a polished cement slab like a dissecting table in the centre of the room. Major Rahman pulled back the white cloth, I noticed automatically that it was the cheapest form of cotton, and revealed Jo's head. It was unmarked but the rest of the body was still covered. A small patch of blood stained the centre of the cloth like an official seal. I'd heard that death brought peace to the features but Jo didn't look peaceful; younger but not calm, not satisfied with death. Less than fifteen hours ago this was my friend, talking and eating like the rest of us, I thought, and the banality of it made me grimace.

'Yes, it's Joseph Katchyan.' I turned away quickly. 'Is that all?'

Rahman became abruptly official.

'Yes, that's all. Just sign here, here and here.' He handed me a Chinese fountain pen and flourished the papers. 'Thank you, we don't need you any more. We'll arrange the funeral. It'll have to be tonight. Where do you think his daughter will want him buried?'

'The Armenian Church,' I replied promptly, thinking only that I had to get out, get away from the cell-like room and the smell of death, get back to Shiuli. I kept thinking that she'd be needing me, then remembered that she didn't know yet, that I'd have to tell her. Rahman seemed no less keen than me to leave the morgue. His manner suggested that he was tired of the whole business. What was one more corpse from the Hill Tracts? A dead Armenian was the same as a dead soldier or tribal guerrilla. We stood at the top of the steps leading down into the morgue, breathing deeply, and he offered me a cigarette. It was a cheap, locally produced brand and I reflected that he must be unusually honest if it was all he could afford. Most army officers smoked imported American cigarettes. I took one gratefully.

'Do you know what he might have been doing in Laxmichari?' The question was asked in a drawl, almost a caricature of nonchalance.

'No idea. I suppose something to do with the road he was building.'

Rahman started to stroll over towards the jeep. Heat shimmered up off its bonnet, distorting the low rounded hills smothered in bushes and creepers which lay beyond the high perimeter fence. I kept pace with him as we crossed the parade ground, a patch of yellow dust from which all life had been trampled and burnt out.

'He wasn't married was he?'

'Never as far as I know. Shiuli's his only relative. In fact he was the last remaining Armenian in Bangladesh.'

Rahman wasn't listening. 'No other children?'

'None. She's only his by adoption.'

'I know. It wouldn't be allowed now; a foreigner and a man at that adopting a Bengali girl.' He seemed to sink into his own thoughts. 'I don't have any children, my wife doesn't want them.' He glanced at me briefly then continued. 'Why should she? Only mess up the house, endless bother, all that feeding and cleaning.' It sounded as though he was repeating someone else's arguments.

I could imagine his wife; educated and bored in one empty Cantonment after another, concerned only that when the next coup took place her husband would have allied himself with the right side. He marched ahead of me and my eyes centred on the dark strip down the middle of his green shirt where sweat betrayed his otherwise immaculate appearance.

'Where's Jo's Landcruiser?' I found myself asking, not because I was interested but because I needed to say something.

He stopped, apparently startled by the question, but the answer came quickly enough. 'It's a write-off. We left it there, couldn't get it out even if we wanted to.'

'You were there then?' Again the question sprang involuntarily to my lips and again it seemed to take him off-balance.

He paused before answering. 'Yes, I was there this morning.' His intelligent face sagged and he looked bitter as though remembering things he'd prefer to forget. Then he straightened his shoulders. 'At least he died quickly, you should be grateful for that. There's no doubt but that death was instantaneous.' He avoided my eyes while he spoke and oddly seemed to derive some comfort from this statement.

The driver came running up from where he'd been sitting under a krishnachura tree. Behind its scarlet flowers and feathery leaves lay the ruins of Pandita Vihara. Only the ground plan of the great eighth-century Buddhist monastery, once ranked beside Nalanda in importance, remained. Enclosed within the Cantonment's defences, inaccessible and abandoned, its shattered walls looked as though they'd been used for shelling practice.

Rahman spoke as I climbed into the jeep. 'I won't accompany you. My driver will take you home. You don't mind, do you?' He seemed anxious. 'Eight o'clock this evening, Armenian Church. If there's any problem phone me.' He handed me his card and I thought he was going to say something else but he stepped back from the vehicle and snapped an order at the driver.

As we drove off, dust billowing out behind us, he did shout something. It sounded like, 'Be careful,' but it was impossible to tell above the noise of the engine. He watched us cross the parade ground and stop briefly at the checkpoint before he turned towards the white-painted offices.

The road led straight across flat land where patches of emerald-green rice seedlings waited for the coming rain. Ahead the clouds were building up, blue-black blocks hundreds of feet high, lumbering in from the Bay of Bengal. The monsoon had arrived.

We tore down the centre of the rutted road towards the coming storm, headlights on and horn blaring; the army makes way for no one. I glimpsed some water buffaloes, frightened by the speeding jeep, plunge into a field of seedlings, trampling them down in their terror. A small market town loomed up; people scattered in front of us as we bore down on them without decelerating.

When we reached the two-mile stretch of the Trans–Asian Highway, built in a fit of enthusiasm in the 'sixties, I made the driver stop and beckoned a rickshaw.

The rhythmic swaying of the rickshaw was calming but it didn't help me decide how to break the news to Shiuli. I was unable to think about anything except the morgue and the seal of blood on the white cloth. *Death was instantaneous—* as though he'd known.

The rain hit; a curtain of water swept up the road towards us accompanied by the crack of thunder and violent flashes of lightning. It came down in solid streams and made it impossible to see more than twenty yards. A few cold drops splashed through holes in the plastic hood and fell onto my shoulders, soaking the thin cotton shirt. The rickshaw driver was drenched, he had neither umbrella nor hat.

We passed New Market, swung right into the maze of alleys and narrow streets which make up the old city and ten minutes later stopped outside the shabby, green-painted doors which give access to the garden and house. The street was nearly knee-deep in water. Green coconut husks and other rubbish span idly round in eddies created by a blocked storm drain. I thrust a fifty-taka note into the rickshaw driver's hand, and not wanting to wait for change jumped out of the machine and pushed open one door. As I did so he began to complain that fifty taka wasn't enough.

I turned on him in a fury and shouted in Bengali, 'It's too much. What do you take me for? A half-wit? You're just like every other bloody rickshawallah in this stinking city. Fuck off!'

In the protection of the doorway a young woman with a baby in her arms watched us mutely. She wore only a cotton sari, too poor to afford even a blouse, and it clung damply to her slight figure. The baby, its eyes outlined with soot from an oil lamp for good luck, stared dumbly at its mother. The rickshaw driver grumbled that it was raining and that it was a long way from the Asian Highway but I ignored his complaints, slammed the door behind me and ran through the garden. Wet plants slapped against my legs and the rain soaked every stitch of clothing in a few seconds. I leapt up onto the veranda where, as I expected, Shiuli sat, with an open book in her lap. Water dripped from my hair and a puddle formed around me on the polished black and white tiles. My anger made me momentarily forget what I had to say to her.

'Charles! Shomela tells me you were arrested by a general. I'm glad he decided to release you,' she said languidly, a smile playing about the corners of her mouth like tiny fish darting nervously at a grain of rice in a pond.

'Jo's dead,' I blurted out, unable to stand her calm. 'He skidded over a ravine last night. The army found him this morning. I'm sorry.'

Her face closed off, the fish darted away and her mouth

formed into a hard line. She looked away from me and out into the garden, her hands motionless on the book. There was no sound other than that of water crashing into the trees, pouring in solid streams off the flat roof and gurgling down the cement channel beside the house.

I walked round behind her and rested my hands lightly on her shoulders, which trembled as though with fever. 'I'm sorry,' I repeated, 'I meant to put it differently. The army wanted someone to identify him, that's why they came. They say he died instantly.'

She shrugged my hands off and went to her room. I followed her into the house. The doors of Jo's room stood open and on an impulse I went in. The fan turned, rustling papers beneath a small terracotta brick from Pandita Vihara. The upward-facing side depicted a woman dancing, one hip thrust out provocatively, warm-fleshed in a bachelor's room full of things which had only had meaning for him. The room seemed smaller than mine or Shiuli's because it was crowded with cupboards and bookcases, while the remaining wall space was taken up with photographs. One next to the door caught my attention. Dated 1947 it was a picture of Jo standing in front of a big open car. He was smiling broadly and had one hand proprietorially on the bonnet. In the background, so faded it was only just discernible, was the outline of an enormous building, a palace even by the standards of Bengal. It was nowhere I recognised. Next to this photograph was its twin; the same except that a woman in a sari had replaced Jo. She was half-turned, about to climb into the car. It was difficult to make out her features but her hair hung loosely to her waist, and one arm was raised as though to ward off the photograph. I switched off the fan and closed the door behind me.

The poor woman I noticed at the gate was on the veranda when I went to find Kamrul, our guard and gardener. She looked about her shyly, clutching the baby tightly to her breast, and she started like a wild animal at my appearance. With wide, frightened eyes she made for the steps again but a sudden flash of lightning drove her back, forcing her to face me. 'Sir, please help me. I need some money to get back to my village. You're a rich man, please help me sir.'

She made as if to touch my feet but I prevented her and motioned her to a chair. She sat upright on its edge and spoke so quietly that I could only just hear her above the thunderous roar of wind and rain. 'My husband came to find work in Chittagong four months ago and sent me a message soon after he arrived with his address. I didn't hear from him again so I came to find him. I went to the address but people there told me he'd married again and left about a month ago. Please sir, I have no more money to get back to my village, please help me.' She wouldn't meet my eyes but desperation, whether the details of the story were true or not, had made her brave.

Glad to have something else to think about and something to do, I heated up the remains of the previous night's curry in the kitchen. I felt disgusted with myself for the way I'd shouted at the rickshaw driver and this was a chance to assuage my guilt. The woman stared at the food hungrily when I put it on the veranda table, but didn't realise it was for her. I gestured towards it and she glanced from it to me, afraid of being tricked, before understanding. She smiled warily, perhaps fearful that I would demand payment in kind later, but for the moment she was hungry and exhausted enough to risk anything. I told her she could sleep on the veranda and I would give her the bus fare in the morning.

Leaving her there I closed the doors of my room and flinging myself down on the bed reached for the cheap wooden box in which I kept a few ganja-filled cigarettes. I muttered angrily to myself. Everything made me angry; that Jo had died so stupidly and wastefully, that I'd had to identify the body, that the army driver had shown his contempt for other people by tearing through the crowded bazars, but most of all the girl on the veranda made me angry.

'What a great man you are,' I said to myself. 'How generous! A pretty girl with big eyes comes to the house so you help her a little and feel good about it. Your conscience is salved and your Boy Scout, paternalistic instinct is satisfied.'

Even this self-abuse was preferable to drowning in the whirlpools of memory.

Gradually the drug relaxed the taut muscles; my attention focussed on a gecko clinging to the ceiling above the fan. It was stalking another, smaller gecko, running a few quick steps and then remaining motionless for minutes on end. The smaller one didn't move, unaware of the danger or transfixed with terror. From four inches the hunter made a rush and clamped its jaws around the other's tail, which fell off as though released by a spring. The tail squirmed in the thing's mouth like an eel on a hook. I turned over in disgust, my thoughts on the casual violence which infects the country and everyone who lives there, like a beggar's leprous sore open to passers-by and flies alike.

3

WE MADE A forlorn gathering a few hours later in the graveyard of the Armenian Church. The rain hadn't let up for a moment and the ground was waterlogged. Four soldiers carried the coffin from Rahman's jeep to the grave which Kamrul had been digging all evening. He'd tied his *lungi* up between his legs and was covered in mud. The grave was too short for the coffin and we stood about silently as he hacked at the sodden earth, standing in the hole he'd already dug. Water poured down his back exposing strips of black skin below the red mud. Mosquitoes buzzed around us, seeming to rise out of the earth itself like spirits from the underworld sent to torment the living.

The soldiers ran back to the jeep outside the walled graveyard, away from the rain and ghosts, leaving Shiuli, Nazmah, Major Rahman, Shomela, Kamrul and myself as the only mourners. Shomela, supported on either side by Shiuli and Nazmah, was unable to stem the tears which dribbled from her rheumy eyes and she moaned quietly to herself, shaking her head.

The graveyard, burdened with premature deaths from disease and childbirth, and overgrown with weeds and small trees, had the atmosphere of all abandoned places: a visible desolation in which it was impossible to feel alone.

Rahman looked incongruous in his jungle fatigues beneath a large black umbrella. He watched Kamrul with a detached air, one hand behind his back and his feet placed slightly apart as though he'd given himself the order to stand at ease. His manner suggested that he was only there to ensure that it was all carried out properly and he occasionally gave Kamrul an abrupt direction, which was studiously ignored. A Petromax in the shade of his umbrella threw ghostly shadows onto the walls and into the pillared side aisles of the church.

When the grave was large enough Kamrul scrambled out and Rahman fetched the soldiers. They grunted as they let the heavy coffin down into the hole, quickly filling up with water, and then withdrew from the alien environment again.

Shiuli, calm and erect, recited a poem by Nazrul Islam from memory, the words falling into the roar of the rain and the Petromax like scraps of paper into a furnace. She dropped an hibiscus flower, blood red and baroque, into the darkness of the grave. Nazmah and myself followed suit.

Shiuli had refused to allow the Roman Catholic priest to officiate, or even be present.

'I don't care what anyone thinks, Jo hated organised religion and I'm not going to make him submit to it now. One of his favourite quotes was from the Sufi Rabia el-Adawia, "I will not serve God like a labourer, in expectation of my wages."'

She'd once told me that when she first went to school, to the Sacred Heart in Andher Killa, the nuns had held religious instruction classes.

'Jo had a big argument with them about this. He rightly said it was bound to be biased towards Catholicism and refused to let me attend.'

'Why did he send you to a Catholic school?'

'Because it was the best one in Chittagong. As you can imagine he had a fight on his hands, those nuns aren't in Bangladesh for the good of their health. Eventually Jo lost but in the evenings he often talked to me about other religions, as an antidote he said.'

Rahman gestured towards Kamrul, who was already shovelling mud and water back into the gaping hole. 'I'll stay and bring him back if you want to leave.'

Shiuli and Nazmah took Shomela with them into the church to make the final entry in the book which had recorded all marriages, deaths, births and christenings in the Armenian community for more than two hundred years. The doors creaked on their hinges as they were unlocked and pushed open. Two naked light bulbs lit up in the high, graceful nave.

Built to hold three hundred people towards the end of the eighteenth century, the church had been virtually unused since the last priest had left. The community had died off or emigrated one by one and for five years Jo had been the sole Armenian left in Bangladesh. The onion-shaped tower was black with pollution, its cross tipped at a drunken angle and bodhi trees had seeded themselves in the stonework; soon their strong roots would break the walls apart and within a decade or two the building would be no more than a pile of rubble surmounted by a writhing mass of grotesque roots and branches.

The women left in Nazmah's Mercedes but I waited, it seemed the least I could do for the last Armenian. Three hundred years of history ending in a muddy hole; no ceremony, no pomp, just a grave and six witnesses. In a few years no one in Chittagong would remember the Armenians. Nothing would remain of them other than a street name and an elegant house or two, falling steadily apart from the depredations of damp and white ants. But then who remembered the Armenians anyway? It was little more than half a century since the Ottoman Turks massacred half the Armenian population of eastern Antolia and Transcaucasia. One and a half million Armenians shot, burnt or starved to death in a few short years.

Jo's family had escaped from Kars on the ancient silk route, joined relatives in what was then East Bengal and put their business acumen to use.

Rahman shifted uncomfortably and slapped a mosquito on his arm. 'Bloody things, can't stand them. We lose more men in the Hill Tracts from malaria than we do from the guerrillas.'

'And the guerrillas?'

'God knows. We don't get many of them.' He looked round dramatically at the soldiers, as though to check that they weren't listening, though we had to shout to hear each other. 'It's a hateful war, but Dhaka refuses to negotiate and I do what I'm told.'

He seemed to wait for comment but I was too surprised by his honesty to say anything and he eventually continued. 'Waste. That's all this war is. Waste of time, waste of money, waste of lives.'

'Why don't you get out? Resign.' I wasn't very interested in his opinions, surprising as they were.

'I can't. Dhaka would regard it as an admission of disaffection.' He stopped abruptly, perhaps aware that he'd compromised himself, and pushed a few clods of earth towards the grave with his polished boot.

The newspapers rarely mentioned the war between the tribal guerrillas, or Shanti Bahini as they liked to be known, and the army, although the foreign press occasionally reported massacres. A week before I'd heard a rumour that three hundred tribal villagers had been wiped out by the army. Nor did people discuss the political situation in the Hill Tracts openly but something prompted me to question him about the rumoured massacre, as though I wanted to walk into a trap, with my eyes open and all my senses alert to the danger.

'What happened at Kalampati?' I asked as Kamrul shovelled the remaining mud into place and patted it down.

Rahman's head jerked up. 'Murder!' He spat the word out so harshly that Kamrul stopped working and stared at him. Rahman's face poked forward at me aggressively, like a vulture about to rip into the swollen belly of a drowned dog, then he turned on his heel and walked stiffly back to the jeep.

I took a last look at the mound over Jo's body. Rain was already wearing channels in the soft earth, levelling Kamrul's work, reducing it to a nondescript patch of mud among the overblown weeds and trees.

Rahman sat motionless in the front passenger seat as we drove through the flooded streets and he didn't turn or even say goodnight when Kamrul and I got out again a few minutes later.

'Whoresons,' Kamrul said, making an obscene gesture in the direction of the jeep's retreating tail lights. 'We fought the Pakistanis only to have them replaced by bastards like that.'

I wondered whether I'd been wise in mentioning Kalampati to Rahman.

Part Two

4

I'D BEEN IN the city for a year and a half, travelling to the University by bus nearly every day and giving a few ill-attended lectures, before I met Shiuli and Jo.

I'd first grown used to such a life in southern Sudan, until I tired of the place and typed out a batch of letters to university English departments in the Indian sub-continent. Chittagong, surely by some never to be repeated clerical aberration, had been the first to offer a post. I flew from Calcutta into the tiny airport at Chittagong in summer and after the Sudan's desert wastes Bengal's countryside seemed like a lush paradise. The patchwork of paddy fields, square water-filled ponds and tiny villages surrounded by trees, held me entranced as I stared from the window of the Fokker Friendship. There seemed to be more water than land, a welcome change, and I felt that I was about to touch something tender and fresh; the soft-mouthed life I'd so missed in the Sudan where unforgiving sand and stars were the only company. As we circled over the city I could see the land rising to the east where the Chittagong Hill Tracts begin and beyond them the higher mountains of Burma and Mizoram. I experienced a pulse of schoolboyish excitement at the thought of jungle, tigers and elephants.

These innocent expectations were shattered the first time I rode a rickshaw up the steep cutting known as Tiger Pass. Two small boys, perhaps seven or eight years old, ran behind, helping to push the rickshaw uphill. Horrified I jumped out. Without my weight the driver was able to pedal easily and the two disappointed boys ran back for another rickshaw.

'Why did you do that?' the driver demanded when I remounted at the top of the slope.

'Because they're children and I don't want to kill them or you.'

'We die from lack of money not from work,' he grunted.

'What's a few *paise* to you? Nothing. Without *paise* we don't eat.'

I met Shiuli and Jo at the Chittagong Club. I disliked the Club but it was one of the few places where it was possible to get a drink and enjoy it without fear of harassment. I wasn't a Club member, it was too expensive for my exiguous salary, but people either assumed I was or were too polite to ask; one of the privileges of being white.

I made a half-serious propitiatory gesture to the two enormous rain trees halfway up the hill as I passed beneath their outflung branches supporting a wealth of parasitic ferns and creepers. At the Club gates the guard, a dignified old man with a sergeant-major's moustache, stood to attention and saluted smartly. I'd stopped telling him that he needn't bother; it was a ritual which he found necessary.

The depression which had driven me from my bare room lifted then, and I nearly turned back, but in one of those flurries of mental activity which throw up reasons for action, I decided that it would render the old man's salute meaningless and spoil his evening if I did so.

There was no one I knew in the brightly lit and ugly bar, so I carried my drink into the garden, regretting it a fraction too late. Mushtaque Islam waved from the far side of the lawn and pulled out a chair for me. He was, as always, impeccably dressed in a dark grey suit, cream silk shirt and a silk cravat. Only a pair of gold and diamond cufflinks spoilt this mercerised appearance and even he seemed to think they might be a little flashy, for he often covered them with his hands. His wife, a fat woman trussed up in a sari like a piece of meat in a sack, sat dumbly beside him, but otherwise they were alone. I only bothered with Mushtaque because Nazmah, his daughter, was my sole friend in the city. I knew from past experience that Mushtaque's wife was so painfully shy that no amount of teasing or seriousness would persuade her to dare more than a meek yes or no and I resigned myself to a dull evening, partially relieved by the view.

We sat beneath a frangipani tree whose stub-fingered branches, elongated leaves and strongly scented, flamboyant blooms stood out grotesquely against a night sky dusted with powdered moonstones. Below us were spread the city's lights and hills. In the distance I could make out the shadows of cranes on the docks and the ghostly silver of the River Karnaphuli sliding by on its way from the Chittagong Hill Tracts to the Bay of Bengal.

Mushtaque's English was perfect but dated, and I derived some amusement from his company by deciding when the particular idioms he employed had fallen out of use in Britain. Luckily his brand of conversation only required me to appear to listen and to nod occasionally.

I was immensely relieved when Nazmah joined us. Although her father was rich enough and willing to support her in idleness Nazmah preferred to work as a lecturer in the University's History Department. I spent much of my time at the University drinking tea in her little office while she expounded her passion: the history of the city and its surrounding hills. In her enthusiastic way, flinging aside mounds of papers to find a book or a quotation, Nazmah invested the city with a past which was not obvious to the casual observer.

She seemed lost in her own recondite historical world and paid little attention to her father, sitting aloof from his dull anecdotes and appearing not to notice when he sought her approval for a story. But his insistent, domineering manner made it impossible for us to talk to each other. I was thankful when he glanced round at a group of men by the bar and stood up.

'Excuse me. I must pop off, I have a little business to attend to.' He smiled apologetically. 'I can never call my time my own.'

'Of course he's guilty,' Nazmah said after her father had gone. The University's Vice-Chancellor had recently been charged with embezzlement and fraud in connection with building contracts on the campus. 'He's as corrupt as most people with aspirations to a Western lifestyle and a salary of only three thousand *taka* a month.'

'But still, fifty lakh taka is a lot of money anywhere. He can't have thought he'd get away with it.'

I'd met the Vice-Chancellor once, a little scarab of a man with a quiet, inoffensive manner. He'd seemed weighed down by responsibility, but perhaps it was only fear of being found out.

'Why not? Most people do. He'll spend a few months in jail, then buy his way out and into some other post with equally lucrative possibilities.' Nazmah spoke English with an indeterminate accent, that of one who has spent as much time in the States as in Britain. Her father's various businesses had taken him and his family all over the world, and by the time Nazmah was twenty she'd lived in more capital cities than most people visit in a lifetime. The study of history and her almost neurotic delving into the city's past I explained in terms of this restless upbringing; she'd been a stranger all her life and even in her native city was something of an outsider.

I offered her and her mother drinks and crossed the lawn, recognising a few faces. A group of British engineers tried to make me join them. They'd had too much to drink and their conversation was drifting onto the shoals of race prejudice. They hated Bangladesh and lived only for the holiday trips to Bangkok.

Sitting at the bar was a man I'd often seen around Chittagong but never spoken to. He had the appearance of an old Bengal hand: dry yellowish skin and an expansive, relaxed manner. I had him down as a retired tea garden manager. On the bar stool next to him was a young Bengali woman. They leant towards each other and were talking in low voices. As a couple they intrigued me. It was rare enough to see a single Bengali woman in the Club but I'd never before seen one in the lone company of a white man. She smoked a cigarette negligently and this too surprised me; even Nazmah didn't smoke in public, though I'd once seen her arrive at the University in her car and climb out holding a cigarette. Many students noticed and stared in surprise or shock at this unladylike behaviour. It took her some time to realise what was wrong but when she did she threw the stub on the ground and, to her credit, laughed in the faces of her audience. The woman's left elbow rested on the bar while her right hand played with six narrow and curiously worked bangles, twisting them round and round absent-mindedly. As I turned from the bar she laughed loudly at something. In the quiet room the laugh had a reckless and raucous ring to it.

'You've not met Shiuli or Jo before?' Nazmah asked as I handed over her whisky.

'Shiuli?'

'Shiuli, the dark woman at the bar with the old man, Jo. I saw you hesitate when you noticed her, then recover yourself and come back to us here.'

'I hardly took her in,' I answered stiffly. 'And only then because she was fiddling with her bangles. Do you know where they came from? I've never seen any like them before.'

'No idea. She was probably given them by some boyfriend in London. She came back a couple of months ago.' The conversation had begun to bore her. Nazmah's appearance didn't interest her and that of others even less so. 'Would you like to meet them? Come on, I'll introduce you and you can get me another drink.' She downed the one I'd just brought, to her mother's horror.

Nazmah stood up and looked around for a moment before spotting what she wanted; an old man standing by himself on the veranda. She greeted him and then brought him down the steps to us.

'A chaperon for mother. Come on, we can leave them now.'

I said goodbye to Islam's wife—I never discovered her name, for Mushtaque invariably ignored her if introductions had to be made—but she hardly listened to me. I felt sorry for her, she couldn't understand her daughter or the world in which she lived. Her husband took little notice of her and I certainly couldn't penetrate the desires, expectations and beliefs of a woman brought up and maintained in ignorance. She'd been taught that her role in life was to sustain her husband, but wealth deprived her of the physical and time-consuming aspects of caring and she was left with only the mental ones, for which she hadn't been trained. It was difficult to see what enjoyment she squeezed out of her existence, other than eating and sharing malicious gossip.

I was a little annoyed with the way Nazmah had disappeared like a genie, leaving me to follow, but I found her at the bar.

We'd been carrying on a desultory flirtation for nearly a year, on her side more in the spirit of a game than I found flattering and on mine ... perhaps to discover whether it was possible to have a relationship with a Bengali woman. It hadn't developed far but we enjoyed each other's company, though she was always conscious of the need to maintain her family's good name in the city.

'You don't understand that riches are only acceptable in this society if they're accompanied by at least a superficial adherence to Islam.' And another time, mischievously, 'It's not me but Chittagong. When we lived in London we used to holiday in the South of France and I wore no more clothes than anyone else—out of sight of my parents anyway. Here I have to pretend.'

As Nazmah introduced me to the two strangers I was struck by Jo's pale blue eyes. Nazmah used to joke that she never heard what Jo said because of the mesmeric effect of his eyes, 'the colour of lightning'. His face had the appearance of a heavily weathered rock, worn by the elements into rounded segments, divided by deep clefts and fissures. I guessed him to be over sixty but he was well-built and his back straight.

Scraps of Jo's conversation come back to me now.

'Born in Narayanganj, schooled in war, educated in love,' he once responded sententiously to the questioning of an inquisitive American, making it sound final, as though there was no need to say more. Yet he wasn't naturally reticent about his life and when he did talk of it I had the impression I was peering into a rusty tin containing a handful of rough, uncut rubies which glittered malignantly.

He liked to remind people of the adventurous spirit of his race. 'We Armenians were here before the British. There's an Armenian gravestone in Calcutta dated 1630, more than half a century before the British claim to have founded the slum.'

And, 'In 1560 the great Akbar made an Armenian called Mariam Zamani his queen.' I never discovered whether it was true or not.

Once—it was early evening and he was shaving in front of a mirror on the veranda—he told us that he thought the Armenian Church should be allowed to fall down. 'Dust to dust and all that. It's more in the spirit of the country. Mud is baked into bricks, a building is put up and eventually those bricks melt back into the mud and river. This passion for preservation is a very Western idea, an attempt to beat off time. Much better to let everything fall down and start again, afresh.'

'That's an engineer talking,' Nazmah had responded sharply.

The contrast between Nazmah and Shiuli was striking. Nazmah was pale, had the sharp, angular features of an Arab and a haughty expression which gave her a daunting look, modified only by her obvious untidiness and extravagant gestures. She didn't really care what people thought of her on first sight, an attribute she shared with Shiuli. She possessed one unusual physical characteristic; the grey-green eyes of a Mamluk. It was this which had first made me notice her at the University. I'd asked a colleague who she was and been given a brief run-down on her family, which ended dismissively with, 'She's a divorcee.' If this was supposed to damp my interest, it only quickened it and I stopped her one day as she hurried past to ask whether there was any history of the city in English. There wasn't but I couldn't have hit on a more fortunate subject and our friendship had grown from that time on.

Shiuli was slight and shorter than Nazmah, with a gentler, oval face, but her features were strongly marked: a wide, full mouth, straight nose and eyes like knots in the teak of her skin, 'peasant black' she called it. The overall impression was one of a sympathetic intelligence, nothing like the obvious cutting edge of Nazmah's intellect. They could have come from different countries, and in a way they did; Nazmah from Bengal's aristocracy of the rich and Shiuli, as I discovered, from the city's slums.

Nazmah talked to Jo and they seemed to get on well. When I knew Jo better I found it hard to understand this friendship, for his bluff good humour and the immediacy of his reactions had little in common with Nazmah's objective, historically based assessments and opinions. They disagreed and argued about everything, especially religion and politics, which Jo hated and Nazmah had a dispassionate fascination for.

Shiuli and I were left to ourselves but once or twice I caught Jo's electric blue eyes watching me over Nazmah's shoulder. The stare, I thought, of a jealous man; I had no doubt but that Shiuli and he were lovers.

Shiuli told me that she'd been in London for seven years, studying Law and practising as a barrister.

'I don't know why I came back. I thought there was something I could do here but now I'm not so sure. Why are you here?'

'Put it down to an unquiet soul. I just happened to end up here—no particular reason to choose Chittagong but I can't say that I don't like it.'

'At least it's stimulating to be surrounded by so much colour, noise, life and death. In London you can exist without knowing you're alive. That's impossible here, your senses tell you you're alive all the time, whether the experience is pleasant or not. You can't drift around in a daze.'

'Yes,' I agreed. 'It's a little like losing your virginity. Once you've lost it you're not the same person but there's nothing you can do about it. You can't go back to what you were before.'

It was a boorish line, one I'd used before on Bengali women, always with the effect of scaring them away. But it was my turn to be surprised.

'I feel the same about London. I was one person when I left and I'm another now,' Shiuli said with a straight face. 'But I did lose my virginity in London so perhaps that's it.'

For a moment I thought I must have misheard, then her serious mask collapsed at my confusion and she spluttered into that unrestrained laugh; throwing back her head and revealing the long line of her throat. A few businessmen at the bar looked up disapprovingly, as though to say that women shouldn't laugh so loudly, or at all.

We talked about London, its pleasures and disadvantages and she told me about her first boyfriend.

'I was twenty-two and never been kissed. I'd never even been out with a man. He was called Frank and was terribly nice in that English way. He took me to the cinema and showed me London but never touched me. I couldn't understand it and thought there must be something wrong with me. He was a big disappointment. We did eventually end up in bed together but it was more my doing than his and I discovered that I knew more about sex than he did. It seems extraordinary. He'd been brought up in a society which initially shocked me with its blatant sexuality but somehow he'd not learnt anything. I did love him for his kindness and generosity though.'

It was difficult for me to take in that this was a Bengali woman speaking. I hadn't come across such unashamed honesty before. Shiuli had broken the conventional restraint surrounding the subject of sex in the first few minutes of our conversation and although she wasn't talking loudly she appeared not to care whether others in the bar heard her or not. Some of my female students, by comparison, hardly dared to speak to me at all, even after eighteen months. While knowing that I preferred Shiuli's forthrightness I was unsure how to take it. In the context of the society I'd been educating myself into, coaxing myself to accept and understand on its own terms, her behaviour was shocking.

Mushtaque joined Nazmah and Jo and soon his loud voice and faintly disagreeable, high-pitched laugh dominated. Shiuli talked about him.

'I used to respect him for what he did during the Liberation War. Instead of leaving the country with his family like most of his class, he fought. He didn't have to, he has enough money to live anywhere in the world, but he stayed. By all accounts he fought bravely too. It's surprising when you look at him now, isn't it? He has, or had, a passion for the idea of Bangladesh and was prepared to put his neck on the line for it. I'm not so sure about him now.'

'And Jo? What's his passion?' I tried to keep my voice sounding casual.

'With Jo it's everything.' She leant forward on the bar stool to bring her mouth nearer my ear. 'At the moment it's his dislike of Mushtaque.' The proximity of her body, a strand of her hair which brushed my cheek and the caress of her whisper made my voice catch in my throat.

'He's right, Mushtaque's a fool.' It was the best I could do. I was overpowered by her physical presence. I carried on quickly, 'He's like a child who expects everything to be done for him, and it is.' I was scarcely aware of what I was saying, so conscious was I of her warm arms extending from the folds of her sari, her smooth skin and the constantly changing pattern of her mouth.

'He's like most men in this country, spoilt by their mothers, sisters and wives; like children they want to possess everything. But Western men aren't very different.'

Behind her Mushtaque was talking about the water lotus, the national symbol.

'It is the spirit of poetry in our national soul, a symbol of purity and brotherhood which has a universal appeal.'

Shiuli scowled and turned to face him as he began to quote the terrible, English translation of one of Tagore's poems. She allowed him to get no further than the exhortation:

> 'Let Love's lotus with its inexhaustible
> treasure of honey
> open its petals in thy light ...'

'I think it's a symbol of neglect and complacency,' she said slowly.

Nazmah widened her eyes in mock horror and glanced at her father. Poetry and nationalism were his favourite subjects.

'When there's flood and famine,' Shiuli continued, 'the poor eat the stalks of the lotus because it's the only food available, and not a very good one. The fact that it's a poetic and nationalist symbol is ironic. It demonstrates the chasm which exists between us, the romantically inclined intellectuals and the rest. We see only the beauty of the flower, a beauty which mocks the millions who go hungry. To them it's a symbol of starvation.'

'No, they see its beauty and are proud of being Bangladeshis,' Mushtaque declared.

'Rubbish. Most of them are too busy trying to survive to care about anything else.'

While Shiuli and Mushtaque argued, Jo talked enthusiastically about the tribal people of the Chittagong Hill Tracts to Nazmah and myself. 'Can you imagine anything more delightful than a people who have a proverb which runs, "As you dance so you reap"? What an incitement to dance! The higher you jump and the more energetic you are the higher and stronger your corn will grow.' He bounced on his stool as though wanting to jump around the room shouting 'As you dance so you reap'. 'Or people who punish elopement by making the offenders buy a pig and give the whole village a feast. How enlightened!'

'They've always been known for their lackadaisical attitudes.' Nazmah's smile robbed the statement of any implied criticism. 'One British official employed Bengalis to teach the tribals how to use the plough and was disappointed but amused when he went to see how they were getting on. He found the tribals smoking and cracking jokes with their backs turned on the Bengalis. "Oh yes," they said, "we're learning very well, soon we'll be able to hold the plough ourselves." That was as far as the experiment got because ploughing involves work and a concept of surplus which was alien to the tribals. Their method of agriculture needed little work and provided a sufficient return.'

In her dispassionate way she went on to explain what was happening in the Hill Tracts. 'It's what's happening to tribal people throughout Asia. Tribal cultures, with their self-sufficient existence are anachronisms in the twentieth century—'

'Even if they're free of the cruelties and vices of modern societies?' Jo interrupted.

'I don't think that they're anachronisms, but they're considered to be so by those with power. In colonial times they were protected by their relative isolation but now, because they've always been outside the mainstream cultures and haven't advanced, whatever that means, into a capitalist or communist mode of production, they make easy pickings for governments and entrepreneurs who only recognise documented land rights. It's historically inevitable.'

'Why are there so many different tribal groups in such a small area, all with different ethnic origins and languages?' I asked.

Mushtaque overheard and broke off his argument with Shiuli. He was a little drunk and swayed on his feet as he spoke.

'Ah, those tribals,' he said, before anyone had a chance to answer my question. 'Their women go round naked, showing off their titties and not caring a toffee who sees. A delight, a delight. I was in Bandarban last week to see about some weaving business. They were all lined up in the weaving shed, naked titties joggling up and down as they worked.' He giggled. 'A lovely sight. Joggle, joggle they went. We'll be able to use it as part of the advertising when we export the cloth; naked titties, hee hee.'

He tried to demonstrate the effect with his hands but sloshed half a tumbler of whisky over the bar instead. Fortunately his wife came in from the garden at that moment, looking cold and lonely. Mushtaque grinned at us fatuously, said, 'Joggle, joggle,' and stumbled towards her.

Nazmah grasped her father firmly by the arm and left with her parents.

'He gets worse every time I see him,' Shiuli said. 'I won't put up with you if you ever become like that, Jo.'

'Nazmah usually does what's expected of her, apart from divorcing her husband of course.' Jo looked at Shiuli half-critically. 'You're a different matter.'

'I'm a different matter because I discovered Marx and believed him for a while. Nazmah is happier writing history than trying to be part of it.'

'And I've never read him,' responded Jo, 'but it's time to go, the bar's closing.'

Shiuli invited me for a drink, then added, 'Or a smoke. Come on, it's far too early to go to bed.'

I hesitated and glanced at Jo but he was already halfway out of the room. While I was intrigued by them and found Shiuli attractive, I had no desire to become involved with another man's lover. It was a path I'd trodden before and one which had cost me dearly.

'It's got nothing to do with him. I live there as well.'

I accepted.

She got down from the bar-stool awkwardly and as I followed her across the room I noticed that she walked with a limp. Her thick, plaited hair hung down below her waist.

Jo drove us down a narrow lane near the red-brick Armoury and into the old city, where I quickly lost my bearings in the maze of alleys. All the shops were locked and shuttered, the streets deserted, apart from a group of khaki-clad policemen furtively smoking *bidis*, and some mange-ridden dogs scavenging in the gutters. He stopped the battered old car in front of a pair of wooden doors, big enough to take an elephant, set in an even higher wall. He hooted once and a minute later the doors were pulled back by a young man who smiled at us shyly.

'Kamrul's been at the ganja again by the looks of him,' said Jo as we drove in and parked. I was to grow fond of Kamrul over the subsequent eighteen months, for he was invariably even-tempered and took a child's delight in tending the big garden, a delight which sometimes brought him into conflict with Shomela whose goat often nibbled at his carefully nurtured and watered flowers.

Through a mass of trees and bushes I made out the lights of a house. We took a narrow path through the garden and came to a dozen steps leading up onto an elegant veranda running the length of the house, Creepers hung down over the veranda's arches and a strong scent filled the air. I asked what it was.

'It's the *shiuli* flower. Don't you know it? Come and have a look.'

'Watch out for snakes,' Jo said from the veranda, 'and goodnight, I'm going to bed.'

I followed Shiuli a little way into the garden until we reached a small tree, no more than ten feet high, covered in tiny, trumpet-shaped flowers. Their stems were bright orange and their mouths strikingly white in the moonlight.

'It only flowers at night. At dawn, as it begins to get warm, they all drop off but tomorrow night, and every night for a couple of months, it will be covered again.'

I drank in the waves of rich scent, thinking that it was almost comically tropical, so lovely and so brief, as insubstantial as romance.

'It's another classic poetic symbol,' she went on, 'the sweetness and transience of love, the pain of its loss. You can imagine. But I shouldn't laugh, it affects me too. When I was in London I began to doubt the reality of this tree and wrote to Jo asking him to send me some of its flowers, but they're too delicate to dry or press. They start to shrivel the moment they're picked.'

I noted that she'd known Jo before she went away but, pushing aside the desire to question her on the subject of their relationship, asked her instead whether her name derived from the tree.

'Of course. From this particular tree in fact.' She patted the thin trunk, causing a few blossoms to fall.

There was little furniture on the veranda, a few worn cane chairs and a cane table. The whitewash was peeling and in places patches of plaster had fallen off, exposing the brickwork beneath. Without the profusion of potted ferns, gardenias, thorns and other plants on the floor and hanging from the walls it would have seemed bleak.

'In the hot season, when Jo's father lived here, they used to hang chick-screens from the roof and employed someone to splash water over them so that whatever the temperature outside it was always cool here. Even now it's not too bad because the house was at least designed for the heat, to catch the slightest breeze.'

I sank into a chair and Shiuli sat cross-legged on the tiled floor.

'It's cooler,' she explained. 'This veranda has one great disadvantage: mosquitoes. Sometimes it's impossible to sit here there are so many of them.'

She rolled some light-green ganja into a cigarette and lit it.

'Did you know it's only the female that bites?' I asked foolishly.

'You're not very good at small talk, are you?' she said by way of a reply, blowing out a stream of smoke.

'Would you prefer to be back in London?' I asked.

'When I'm in this house I'm happy and I've no wish to go back, but most of the time I miss the friends I made and the sense of freedom. Nazmah is the only real friend I have here, she understands how claustrophobic I feel. People can't leave women alone, they notice what we do and condemn it automatically.'

Not then, but some time in the course of the evening, I asked her how she came to be living with Jo.

'I was born out there, on the wrong side of walls like the one around this garden. It's one reason why I'm not accepted by Chittagong society. Although the main one is because we're regarded as a bad influence.'

'Why?'

'For instance, when my schoolfriends' parents were trying to marry off their daughters Jo told me to do anything but get married until I'd travelled a bit, lived in another country— the North Pole if I liked. This was regarded as subversive and immoral.'

'How long have you known Jo?'

'All my life. I was abandoned on this veranda when I was a baby. Jo adopted me.'

I must have looked relieved, because Shiuli laughed and said, 'I thought there was something odd, restrained about you. I'd just decided that you were hard to get through to. English in fact. Perhaps we can start again now.'

I slipped out of the chair and sat a few feet away from her

on the cool tiles, my back resting against the table. We talked, laughed and smoked for hours, until the alcohol and ganja made us too sleepy to continue.

As the sky faded from the indigo of night to dawn silver, Shiuli led me through the house. The walls of the central room were covered in framed photographs: portraits, family groups, the ubiquitous successful tiger hunt. I stopped in front of a large portrait of a bearded man in a black cowl. Cobwebs hung across the corners of the frame.

'Vazken of Echmiadzin, Supreme Catholicos of all Armenians. Jo wanted to take it down but it's been there for as long as I can remember and I threatened to cut my hair in retaliation if he moved it.'

'It sounds as though he's easily persuaded.'

'Not at all. Cutting my hair is a last resort. I've never actually done it. He's always insisted that I should keep it long. He says it's more Bengali.'

Sometime during the evening she'd loosened the plait and now her hair was spread across and down her back in thick black ripples, inviting as a cool pond on a close afternoon. I was tempted to touch it, and put my hand out before thinking better of it.

'He still complains of having to eat his breakfast with God's representative looking suspiciously over his shoulder.'

The furniture was solidly colonial in style, comfortable and imposing. Glass-fronted cupboards concealed one wall, stretching up to a ceiling supported by thick, teak beams twenty feet above us. The cupboards were filled with books in English, Bengali and what I took to be Armenian, their leather bindings cracked and crumbling.

'No one can read the Armenian any more; Jo can speak it but he never learnt to read it.'

The bedroom's windows overlooked the garden and a flight of emerald-green parakeets shot by, wheeling up into the sky and screeching as they went. I arranged the mosquito net carelessly and as I fell asleep heard the Imams calling the faithful to prayer and the crows, beginning to wake up, giving each other laconic early morning greetings.

5

THE UNIVERSITY KEPT me busy for a few weeks, and the next time I went down to Number 1, Armenian Street I found Shiuli and Jo packing things into a new, white Toyota Landcruiser.

'We're going to Cox Bazar this afternoon,' Shiuli told me.

I'd heard about the seventy miles of beach to the south of Chittagong but had never been there.

'Jo's got a new job with Tarmad, the Australian consultants on the road building project in the Chittagong Hill Tracts.' She patted the Landcruiser. 'This is one of the perks.'

As before I was charmed by her unselfconscious enthusiasm but found myself unusually reserved in her presence.

'Why don't you come with us?'

'I have to work unfortunately.' I wanted to go but perhaps sensed that in one way or another Shiuli would upset the easy rhythm of my life. I had achieved a stable and undemanding friendship with Nazmah, an equilibrium in my work at the University which, while not intellectually demanding, was enjoyable, and entry into the higher echelons of Chittagong society by virtue of my colour. At the other end of the scale the old brothel in Nala Para, run by an enormously fat and torpid Anglo-Indian called Sara, served its purpose. I'd come to accept my visits to Sara's establishment as a necessary part of life in the city and had lost the fear and self-digust which assailed me the first time I walked under the arched doorway above which it was still possible to read the English words, 'Forbidden to All Ranks', flaking like dead skin from the damp, diseased wall. Thus, although not perfect, there was no reason to want to change anything; to drift, to enter another culture and to move on when bored, seemed a reasonable, even enviable existence. I guessed that Shiuli, whether as friend or lover, would be more exigent than anyone I'd known in the past.

'No one will notice or even mind if you're away for a few

days,' she pressed.

It was true but I still declined, telling myself that I had a responsibility to the few students who bothered to make the tedious and uncomfortable journey from the city to the University.

'If you change your mind we'll be there for a week, camping about ten miles down the beach.'

She gave me a few unripe mangos as I left, placing them carefully in a basket and smelling each one as though to recapture the humid imprint of the hot season. 'A client brought me dozens from Sri Lanka the other day. We can't possibly eat them all, but it's a treat to have reminders of summer in the dry season.'

* * *

The week began normally, but on the Wednesday the nation's students took to the streets in protest against martial law. The police used tear gas and fired on a crowd in Dhaka, killing three. It was rumoured that over a thousand people had been arrested. All universities and colleges were closed immediately, *sine die* as the newspapers put it.

The next morning I boarded a bus for Cox Bazar, driven both by the desire to see Shiuli and the need to escape Chittagong's foreign community which had showered me with invitations to parties. I'd been to one or two when I first arrived in the city but had soon tired of the suburban back-biting and unconscious race prejudice. The foreigners lived in exclusive ghettos and their sole contact with Bangladeshis was as servants or officials. Almost the only one I liked was Poplavsky, the Russian Consul. He was undoubtedly an alcoholic and probably a spy, but he at least understood something about the country and didn't enter into the standard conversations about the difficulty of finding trustworthy servants. I once gave him a tee-shirt with 'USA' emblazoned across the front, enjoying his badly concealed horror and stammered thanks.

Nazmah was planning a trip to Calcutta, her most and my

least favourite city. There was nothing to hold me.

The bus sped down the rutted road between cracked fields, throwing up clouds of dust, past villages hiding in the shade of fruit trees and bamboo stands, like shy children. Vehicles shot by in the other direction, seemingly engaged in a game of chicken on the narrow, built-up road. A truck full of sand, with a line of labourers like embalmed mummies standing in the back, scraped the side of the bus, nearly nudging us over the embankment. The passengers shouted at the driver to slow down and he did reduce speed until we reached the ferry over the River Matamuhuri. Once across, he resumed the same breakneck pace.

On the ferry I bought a *dab*, green coconut and the vendor deftly sliced off the top with three or four machete blows. Next to me a tall, middle-aged man in Western clothes was drinking from a *dab* with extreme grace. In order to prevent drips falling on his clothes he stood on tiptoe and bet forward at the waist as he upended the heavy nut. His face had been deeply scarred by smallpox and his curly hair was unfashionably and untidily long.

'*Dab* is of course much superior to Coca-Cola,' he said without preliminary. 'It can be used as a drip feed directly into the veins in cases of dehydration caused by cholera.'

Slightly taken aback by this unlikely piece of information, I asked whether he was a doctor.

'No, I am a journalist by profession. You are perhaps the English Professor at the University. I have seen you there thrice.'

'Not a professor, merely a lecturer.'

'And how do you find our students?'

'The students are fine but the course is absurd. People who speak English as their first language have trouble with Shakespeare, Milton and Pope. How students who hardly understand modern English are supposed to cope with them I can't imagine.'

'Our education system is still in a muddle from the British time.' He pushed a thick lock of hair behind an ear but it fell back again almost immediately. 'At present however our students have other things on their minds. But how I love your Shakespeare; Harry Hotspur,

> "Who lin'd himself with hope,
> Eating the air on promise of supply,
> Flattering himself with project of a power
> Much smaller than the smallest of his thoughts;
> And so, with great imagination
> Proper to madmen, led his powers to death,
> And winking leap'd into destruction."'

Again and again I'd come across Bangladeshis who could recite poems they'd learnt as students.

Hardly able to remember two lines for a week myself, this ability to recall great chunks of poetry never ceased to amaze me.

'I'm impressed.'

'That is nothing. I do not want to and cannot recite the *Koran Sharif* from beginning to end without a mistake, but there are many who can.'

I poured some refreshing *dab* juice down my throat, staring up into a liquid aquamarine sky where a vulture floated effortlessly, watching and waiting for a death.

'Islam gets a bad press in the West. To begin with your people felt more at home with Moslems than with Hindus because the religions have more in common.' He glanced at me uncertainly. The scars paralysed his face and gave a terrible displaced quality to the one eye I could see. 'Am I lecturing you?'

'No. What happened? The Mutiny?'

He smiled. 'Yes, the Mutiny or as some of us prefer to call it, the First Independence War. It all depends on your point of view; rebels or freedom fighters, traitors or heroes? The few who attacked the Chittagong Armoury in 1930 and freed the city for a time were hung by your judges. Twenty-five years later we won Independence and we celebrate them as martyrs.'

I handed my empty *dab* to the vendor who split it open, sliced off a thin wedge and gave it back. I used the wedge as a spoon to scrape out the slippery, translucent flesh on the inside of the nut. 'But you had to fight for your freedom all over again in '71.'

'Oppression is a strange word and often strangely justified. Liberation from the Pakistanis only meant freedom for our middle class. Look around you.' He gestured across the wide river at a Nilotic cargo boat so laden with bricks that the thick water rippled within an inch of its freeboard. Its sails were furled, useless in the still air, but five men, as black as the boat's caulking, trudged along the bank bent under a rope which stretched from the top of the mast to their straining shoulders. 'Those men—how far have they come? How far must they go? What have they eaten today? For the majority of Bangladeshis oppression remains a fact of life. When we all perceive that clearly there will be true liberation.'

'You speak like a prophet, you can't be sure that it will ever happen.'

'However, I have faith.'

'You may not like it when it comes.'

'That's true. Certainly I shall not like some of it, but if we can rid ourselves by *jotedhars* and *goondars* I shall be able to console myself. Change is necessary in any country which could feed itself but in which most people are permanently malnourished.'

The ferry crashed into a battered iron pontoon and was swiftly made fast. People jumped ashore and the bus engine roared to life. He handed me his card before returning to a seat at the opposite end of the bus. It read in Bengali and English, 'Abu Zafar Hashim, Editor', followed by the name of his newspaper and several telephone numbers.

As soon as we reached Cox Bazar I started southwards down the beach towards Teknaf. Five children joined me and tried to sell me shell necklaces, cowries and chunks of coral. Even when they understood that I wasn't interested they stayed, asking questions about Chittagong and London. They were as attractive and bright as most Bengali children, with quick smiles and a sharp sense of humour despite their obvious malnourishment. After a mile or so they suddenly presented me with four necklaces, making me feel mean and guarded, and turned inland. They stopped once to wave and shout, 'Bye bye', then clambered over a sand dune and I lost sight of them among the casuarina trees.

✢ ✢ ✢

'Just in time for a drink,' Jo said as I walked into their camp some hours later, and handed me a can of Tiger beer. 'Ha! You were talked into buying those damn necklaces as well, were you? I leave with dozens every time—can't resist the children, that's the trouble.'

I didn't say that I hadn't paid for them.

The Landcruiser was parked in the shade of a group of saplings which sprouted unsteadily from the sand. Clear water cascaded over the cliff and into a pond before flowing down a deep channel to the sea. Along the top of the cliff jungle trees, creepers and bushes competed for space and light, appearing from below as a jagged green line pressed between the flat, red cliff-face and blank sky. The beach stretched tens of miles in both directions, disappearing into a haze of blue and white. Jo took in my dizzy wonder and thirst and turned his attention back to the fire he'd been tending.

Shiuli ran clumsily up from the sea. Once again she surprised me—she was wearing a bikini. Even in this empty place I couldn't imagine any of the other Bengali women I knew being so daring.

'You found us,' she said, settling herself onto the sand. 'Isn't it glorious? The sand's boiling between here and the sea, but you must know that. How long did it take you to walk here?' The words tumbled out irrepressibly, questions and statements thrown together at random and constantly punctuated by the laugh I'd begun to love. 'Do you know that phrase of Tagore's in which he says that individuals only achieve significance when they're alone in the vast empty spaces of nature, where their souls can expand into the universe? That's how I feel here, primal and a part of nature, not separate from it.'

I was disappointed by the water which, far from being the clear tropical blue promised by the tourist brochures, was a murky grey caused, so Jo told me, by the millions of tons of silt brought down from the mountains of Kashmir, Nepal and Tibet. Washed out into the Bay of Bengal, it discoloured hundreds of square miles of sea.

In the evening Jo and I grilled some white-fleshed pomfret we'd bought from an old fisherman who appeared out of the haze, plodding slowly up the beach carrying a woven basket and with a net strung over one shoulder. His skin was coal black and his *lungi* so old as to be almost colourless. He stopped when he reached us and accepted a drink of water.

'Are your fish for sale brother?' Jo asked.

It took the man a second to understand, to realise that Jo, a foreigner, had spoken Bengali, Chittagonian in fact, the difficult southern dialect. When he did understand his uncomprehending shrug froze and he grasped Jo's hand, almost weeping with emotion. At first he refused to accept any payment for the fish. 'A gift to my friends.'

'But uncle,' Shiuli said, 'we have money and we'll be offended if you don't take it. If you like it's for your children or grandchildren, not for you. If you won't take it then we won't take your fish and you'll have to walk all the way to Cox Bazar to sell them.'

We'd already established that the five fish in his basket constituted the entire day's catch and his sole source of income. He stayed until dusk and even then couldn't tear himself away immediately but kept coming back to say something or to pour the blessings of Allah on our heads.

Shiuli wouldn't touch the soft-boned fish.

'The best fish in the world, with the possible exception of fresh tuna. You don't know what you're missing. That monk of yours has a lot to answer for,' Jo told her between mouthfuls.

Shiuli grinned at him, 'You know I was a vegetarian long before I met Boddhipal.' She turned to me. 'Years ago, at the end of the Ramadan fast, I went out for some reason, without thinking. It was early morning, the time when all the cows, goats and chickens are slaughtered for Eid ul-Fitr. The streets were literally running with blood, gutters full of it. Piles of entrails lay everywhere, fought over by dogs and crows. It still makes me shiver to think about it. I don't go out at Eid now, and I've been a vegetarian ever since.'

'Who's the monk Jo mentioned?'

'Boddhipal, a Buddhist Chakma from the Hill Tracts. He runs a small monastery and school in Chittagong; a lovely man. I spend a lot of time with him.'

This was the first I heard of Boddhipal Bhikkhu, who was to play such an important role in the events which followed Jo's death.

*   *   *

The days we spent on the beach together passed too quickly, and are reduced in my memory to daytime heat and light reflected off sand and sea, and evenings when there was nothing but the sound of the ocean beating rhythmically like a *tabla* on the damp sand, as though desiring a more playful union with the delta. Within the ruffles of surf we watched plankton spark alive and then fade away or vanish in a swirl, swallowed up by the maw of water. The only other people we saw were three pitifully thin children with the reddish hair caused by malnutrition. Each morning they led their family's two cows to some scrubby grass growing on the sand dunes further south, and back again in the evenings. They were Hindus from a low-caste fishing village and Jo astonished them by recounting tales from their *Mahabharata*. Gathering round, they would prompt him to tell one of the familiar stories, sitting wide-eyed with wonder and never interrupting. When it was finished they would jump up and rush down the beach after their bony cows. In the evenings they brought him garlands of flowers or shells they'd picked up during the day.

On the third and last morning they found Jo sitting behind an array of glasses, empty bottles and beer cans, Shiuli behind what was left of the dry ice, lentils and powdered milk and myself behind some cooking pots. They approached warily.

'What is it? What are you doing?' asked Shanti, the oldest of them.

'It's a shop,' Jo replied.

'We haven't any money.'

'What do you have?'

'Nothing.'

'What about those shells and flowers you bring every night?'

It took them a moment to comprehend that it was a game, then they went mad; gathering handfuls of shells and rapidly making bracelets of flowers. They took it very seriously, delighting in our childishness, and considered our prices carefully.

'Excuse me sir, I'd like to look at that pot,' the boy Hari said to me, speaking slowly and carefully, as if for a small child.

I feigned the habitual indifference of shopkeepers. 'Which one?'

He pointed. 'How much is it?'

'It's an excellent pot, brother, foreign made. It will last years, not like some of the cheap rubbish that's around nowadays.'

'Maybe but how much is it?'

'Twenty-five shells only.'

He whistled. 'Twenty-five shells! That's expensive for an old pot like this. Look, I can see it's been used; it's burnt on the bottom and scratched inside. I'll give you no more than two shells and a bracelet.'

'Two shells! *Baprebap*! You insult me. It cost me twenty-two. If I sell it for twenty-five I'll hardly make any profit. I've got a family to support,' I indicated Jo and Shiuli, but the boy shrugged. 'You're a hard man but for you I don't mind; twenty-three shells.'

He began to walk away. 'I can't afford such high prices.'

'Wait! Wait sir. As you're my first customer today I'll let you have it at a loss. Twenty shells only.'

'No more than five.'

'Fifteen and two bracelets.'
'Six.'
'Ten and a bracelet.'
'Six.'
'Ten.'

'*Thik acche*.' He paid me and turned to Jo who was busy bargaining with Shanti and her little sister Mira, making them giggle uncontrollably.

Within half an hour everything was sold and the children ran home with their booty, leaving the cows to fend for themselves. Jo and myself had amassed fortunes in shells and bracelets.

'You two are mean,' Shiuli commented. 'Haggling like that and making them pay so much. The unacceptable faces of capitalism.'

'But my dear,' Jo responded with dignity, standing in front of her and pouring his wealth at her feet, 'we only do it for you.'

'You think you can buy me so easily?' she mocked.

I added my shells and flowers to the pile. 'Everyone has their price.'

She threw a handful of sand at me and chased me down to the sea.

The children returned carrying presents of sweet *paish* and an earthenware pot full of toddy from their amazed mother. We shared the *paish* with them, transferred the toddy to a water bottle and sadly said farewell to Shanti, Hari and Mira.

6

Jo and Shiuli went back to Chittagong as they had planned, but Jo convinced me that I should visit the Hill Tracts. He gave me the name of a guide and even seemed jealous of the prospect of my being able to go in on foot. He had only ever done it in a big party, with elephants and bearers and the pomp of Empire.

I checked into an hotel in Cox Bazar and went in search of Jo's contact, Harun Kabir. I planned to spend a week more in the area and Jo had told me that it was possible to visit some of the tribal villages with this man. I tracked him down in a dark tea shop off the main street, directed there from his house by a woman who talked to me from behind a curtain and sent a little girl through with a cup of tea and a biscuit. The tea shop was almost evilly filthy, and I hesitated about drinking anything there, but the tea was scaldingly hot. Harun had a wrinkled, walnut coloured face and narrow, well-manicured hands which he laid on the table between us like gifts to be admired.

'It is difficult now; the army is not liking tourists going to these villages.' He loosed each word reluctantly from his thin lips.

'But it's possible?'

'It is very much possible. If we are spending five days we can go to two villages, maybe three. They are Mru peoples, most different from other tribals and most backward. They are in most undeveloped ruts.'

We made a few practical arrangements and I shook his dry, bony hand.

Dawn the next day saw us leaving the beach and entering the damp lacerated jungle which covers the coastal strip. Our packs, heavy with five days' worth of food, were capped bizarrely with a chicken each, tied securely into place.

'These people are poor,' Harun had told me. 'They have enough for themselves but nothing for visitors. We must take some rice, lentils, vegetables and two chickens as presents.'

Nothing moved apart from the mist which coiled and writhed as we disturbed it, like some giant, ghostly snake. The dense trees and creepers cut out the light and we seemed to be walking in an aquatic environment of greyish blues and greens, sometimes startled into life by a violent red or yellow flower. The path was flat and of hard, well-trodden earth.

'This is not the real jungle. We are not reaching it until this afternoon.'

It looked authentic enough to me but it gradually broke down into empty fields and barren vegetable patches, stitched together by thin, mud barriers. The land was unirrigated and cracked, thirsting for water.

We passed through a Bengali village of thatched houses and neatly swept yards. Women, collecting water from a pond, turned their faces away as we approached and pulled their thin saris up to cover their heads, though one or two peeked bravely and giggled after we'd passed. In the distance the Chittagong Hill Tracts rose in blue waves and far behind them the higher Chin Hills of Burma.

By midday the edge of the true jungle had come to meet us. We rested under a banyan tree overspreading an area the size of three tennis courts, where leaf monkeys leapt distractedly around in the mass of hanging roots and branches, their long tails following them like plumes of smoke. They regarded us inquisitively, the dark grey ruffs surrounding their pale, rufous faces giving them a permanently surprised expression.

A river swung sluggishly around the base of the banyan in a wide arc and the water was temptingly cool.

'Are there crocodiles?'

He kept his eyes closed. 'Not here.'

I stripped and had waded in up to my chest before Harun sprang to life and shouted at me to stop. 'This most dangerous place. You must not be swimming.'

'You're joking.' It couldn't have looked less dangerous.

'I no joking.'

'I felt an almost overwhelming desire to ignore him, to

strike out for the other bank, but he seemed genuinely agitated so, with poor grace, I returned to the shallows.

'What's the problem? The water's slow, you say there aren't any crocodiles, what is it?'

'Englishman drowning here.'

'Here? Perhaps he couldn't swim.' It was impossible to take the assertion seriously. 'Or perhaps it was during the monsoon.'

He began to hack at some dense secondary growth a little upstream with his machete. 'You no believing me? Here, here, look see.'

I watched the river, like green olive oil, slipping past. At that moment animism seemed an eminently sensible faith. The river and the tree were certainly as mysterious and unknowable as any god; to postulate that every river, every tree, animal and rock had a spirit was an immense idea which ramified endlessly, like smells which retouch the colours of childhood.

'You looking here.' Harun stood triumphantly beside a flat rock, holding back the branches so that I could read the words carved into it.

'In memory of our dear friend and colleague, John Aubrey Hutchinson, who vanished while swimming near this spot, aged twenty-seven. 12 February 1924. May he Rest in Peace.'

It was like a slap across the face to find this bald statement in a place miles from anywhere. To think that other Englishmen had not only passed by this spot but had even died here. My frivolity left me and I pressed Harun to move on.

The village was another five hours distant and the path, more like a dry watercourse, climbed and descended steeply. Loose sand crumbled under our feet. It was an exhausting walk, one north-south ridge after another. We waded through small streams and once a rope-way took us over a gorge. It swung wildly as we crossed, one at a time, and the hand-ropes fell outwards disconcertingly when I put too much weight on them. A tree far below looked to be covered in large white flowers until Harun shouted and they exploded into the air as one, resolving themselves into dozens of egrets with black beaks and spindly black legs. Once we heard an animal plunging away into the bush, a wild pig or a deer.

I was so absorbed in contemplation of the extraordinary plants and butterflies, some as big as birds and dangerous-looking, that I didn't notice the soldiers until I was on top of them. They materialised from the jungle: camouflage uniforms, forage caps and automatic rifles. I was in front of Harun and stopped with a jolt, shocked by their sudden appearance.

'Where are you going?'

I gave the name of the village automatically, my heart beating as though I was under sentence of death.

'How long are you planning to spend there?'

'One night and then on to another village.'

'Are you a missionary?'

I laughed but they remained stern-faced and unsmiling so I said, 'No.'

'Do you have any bibles?'

'What?'

'Bibles, do you have any?' He spoke good English and wore a captain's stripes.

I relaxed a little. If they were only worried about priests and liberation theology, then there should be no problem. 'None. You can look if you like.'

He nodded so I unshouldered the pack and after carefully untying the chicken he searched through my clothes and the food before politely repacking it. They ignored Harun, a familiar face perhaps.

'What nationality?'

'British.' I half-expected him to continue: Are you married? How many children? Are your mother and father alive? How much do you earn? The endlessly dull, familiar questions by which people are judged and categorised in peasant-based societies.

'You may stay one night only. You must come back on this path tomorrow. No other villages.' He waved us on like a traffic policeman and they stepped back into the shadows.

Angered by the arbitrary curtailment of my expedition I

started to protest, but then reflected that they could send us straight back if they wanted to, and with an ill-tempered grunt continued down the path.

'Are they always there?'

'Always. Not just in the same places but somewhere around about. They are checking the identity cards of all tribals.'

'Identity cards?'

'All tribals must be carrying identity cards.'

'Why?'

'They are dangerous peoples. They are fighting and they kill soldiers.'

'Do they ever cause you trouble?'

'Oh no, not at all. I bring tourists and they are welcoming me. They are most fond of me.'

The village was an impressive array of rectangular *machangs* ten feet off the ground, supported on solid bamboo poles lashed together with split cane. They had thatched roofs and were perched on the shoulder of a hill overlooking a sea of jungle to the south. They were neatly made and regularly spaced in two lines, one above the other. Notched tree trunks led up onto the *machangs* and banana trees grew next to most of them, their pendulous purple flowers hanging down like grossly engorged sexual organs. Bamboo stands surrounded the village on every side.

Some bristly black hogs slept in a pile beneath one of the *machangs* and water buffaloes stood passively in the shade. A naked child stopped halfway down a ladder when she saw us, let out a wail and scrambled back into the safety of the house. Two women were husking rice in a hollow log, their short black skirts swinging sharply with each blow. The skirts, held up by closely woven silver belts, were split down one side and had narrow red borders which sliced the surrounding greens and khakis as cleanly and unexpectedly as flesh is by razor grass.

Harun shouted and waved his arms in fear at a well-fed dog which sniffed up to us. It gave him a bemused look and loped off. 'These Mru kill a dog when its master dies. They are believing that as it was helping its master in life so it can also be helping him afterwards. Such foolish peoples.'

I was surprised that they should kill dogs or believe in an afterlife of such physical dimensions. 'Aren't they Buddhists?'

'They are most primitive and uncivilised. Once a year they are also killing a cow most barbarously.'

Harun called out to the women in their language and grinned at them wolfishly, showing his red-stained gums and teeth rotted by the *pan* which he chewed constantly, spitting bloody gouts into the dust as he walked. The women didn't smile back or stop working but one of them pointed vaguely behind her. Harun led me to a *machang* and, dropping his pack, climbed the ladder, beckoning me to follow. I hesitated about leaving my camera, passport and other valuables in the open but Harun insisted that they would be safe.

'Thievery is unknown here. Even the women cannot be thieved.'

His attitude towards the Mru seemed to be one of contempt tempered by an uneasy admiration.

The structure shook as we climbed up and a man's voice called out from inside. Harun answered and received a grunt in response. I thought with pleasure that perhaps the Mru were less fond of him than he believed.

The ladder led onto a wide platform in front of a single large room, dim and smoky, though sunlight spliced cracks in the woven walls and scattered itself across the floor, which creaked as we moved across it. Three men squatted behind spherical earthenware pots set in circles of rope to prevent them falling over, sucking vigorously through bamboo straws. A woman stood up from where she'd been winnowing rice, a child at her breast. She was dressed the same as the two outside but had, in addition, a necklace made up of dozens of strands of black beads and another of white cowrie shells. Bangles rattled round her wrists and silver, trumpet-shaped studs distended the lobes of her ears. She made a welcoming gesture and said, '*Namushkar.*' We replied in kind and she and Harun talked.

Unable to understand a word, I looked around. The men and the woman were tall and muscular, with smooth dark skins and wide flattened faces, but where I'd expected to see slanted eyes theirs were horizontal, unlike the few tribals I'd seen in Chittagong and the University. The spacious room contained no furniture, though bedding was rolled up against one wall. Clothes, bananas and what looked like a flitch of bacon hung from a number of bamboo cross-beams. The stench of pigs and shit wafted up from below the house where, it seemed, all refuse was dumped indiscriminately.

'She says you can be sleeping here if you are wanting to. I am always staying in another house.'

I jumped at the chance to be separated from him.

'In another house you could be having womens. Even young girls are thinking nothing of sleeping with anyone. They are beauties isn't it? I know most beautiful girls, most young for you.'

'I don't want her.'

He looked upset. 'But tourist man always has girl.'

'Well I don't.'

One of the men beckoned me and I squatted beside him. He was incapably drunk but friendly and gentle and he showed me how to suck through the bamboo straw. He encouraged me to take as much as I wanted, indicating that he'd had more than enough. At the first suck I nearly choked, for the pots didn't contain beer as I'd imagined but some kind of spirit. The pot was half-empty and I asked with signs whether he'd drunk it all. He nodded vigorously, rummaged among the bedding behind him and produced two green cheroots, six inches long and half-an-inch thick. He presented me with one and picked a smouldering twig from the fire to light them with. The rank cheroots combined with alcohol made our heads spin, a fact which my new friend acknowledged cheerfully by making circular motions with his index finger, laughing and nodding his head of fine hair, held neatly in place with a red comb. He pointed to himself and said '*Iricha Mru*,' so I told him my name. That seemed to finish conversation for a while and we puffed on our cheroots in a companionable silence.

I wandered outside onto the platform and, catching sight

of a pagoda roof amongst the trees nearby, climbed down to investigate. The temple was in a bad state of repair; sections of the once-tiled roofs had been patched with rusty corrugated tin and the wooden structure was rotten although much of the carving remained almost intact—whorls and deep curves like the stylised clouds which provide the background to Tibetan *thanka* paintings. Only the highly polished brass statues of the Buddha, lined up inside like sentinels, were undamaged and complete in themselves. An old monk sat in the shrine chanting and the cadence of repetitions welled solemnly out of the dark interior.

I sat on the steps of the temple and thought about Shiuli. 'She's Bengal as she should be,' I told myself, 'inviolable and unwilling to compromise.' How could I fail to be sucked into the vortex of someone who defied and challenged her own culture at every step? Someone who refused to take its values as her own? Especially when such nonconformism was both dangerous and isolating. A week seemed a long time to be separated from her. I thought about the way she cast a net into the clear sky of her mind and recovered it filled with ideas as marvellous as flying fish. I remembered the few times our skins had touched, passing a current of desire through me like a shock.

By the time I roused myself from this reverie dusk and a smoky blue haze had crept in amongst the trees, scenting the air. Fireflies danced at the edge of the bamboo stands, like reflections of the stars which were beginning to transpire through the skin of the night. The monk was still chanting and it felt as though the deities of the jungle, fascinated and attracted by the serene recitation of Pali poetry, had crowded into the monastic grove to listen.

Harun rushed up to me as I strolled back through the village, which was no more busy than it had been when we arrived.

'Where have you been? Those people were saying they no knowing where you are. They no good people, drunkard people, you will not be staying with them.'

'But I've decided that I will. I like them.'

He skulked off while I carried my pack and sorry-looking chicken up the ladder and presented all the food to the woman. She accepted it with many smiles and a stream of unintelligible words.

There was a party in progress, more men and a few women squatted behind the earthenware pots drinking and talking.

Iricha made space for me beside him and I was soon busy with another cheroot. I was able to observe the currents of conversation without being disturbed by the restraints of language; to understand the spirit if not the meaning. Iricha told a long story which seemed to be against himself and he was frequently interrupted by comments and laughter. The women, although working, took as much part in the laughter and discussion as the men and I felt relieved to be in a place where the two sexes could act normally towards each other, without any of the fluttering eyelashes and false modesty of most of the Bengali women I came across.

A woman squatted down between me and Iricha. She introduced herself in fluent Bengali and informed me that as the guest I had the right to choose what animal should be killed and eaten.

'Anything?'

'Yes. Pig, buffalo, cow, chicken, anything.' She spoke quickly and easily, without shyness, staring directly into my eyes and smiling often. Her long hair was pulled severely back, as though to emphasise the plumpness of her face.

I decided on chicken as that was what I'd brought and it was obviously the least valuable. The woman's name was Naiz and I asked her about the ceremonial sacrifice of a cow which Harun had mentioned.

'Turai, who created all things, sent the Mru people their holy text written on a banana leaf. The messenger was a cow but on the way it felt hungry and ate the leaf. That is why we have the *Kumlang*, to punish the cow for eating our holy book.'

'I thought you were Buddhists.'

'We are Buddhists but that doesn't mean that we have to abandon our gods or traditions, the two are separate. We would no longer be Mru without such things.'

My drink-fuddled mind could make little sense of this but she went on.

'It is like dancing. We dance because we are Mru, not because we are Buddhists, but we are still both. Once a year the young of the village spend a night in the jungle dancing and singing. The girls and the boys. They dance for Turai, for Sung-Tung the god of the hills, for Oreng the river god, and they dance to represent the spirits of the wild trees in the forest, the crops suckling at the sun, and the animals hunting in the shadows of the night. The only thing that Mru of this village do not represent is the mango tree, for we are said to have been born of it ourselves and it would bring bad luck—'

She was interrupted by the appearance of Harun who'd come to confirm my decision to stay where I was. He was greeted uproariously by the men who offered him sucks from their spirit pots. No sooner had he excused himself from drinking at one than another would be proffered, forcing him to explain his religious objection to alcohol each time. The men seemed to find the concept unbelievable and risible. He took the joke in good part but obviously found it a little wearing and didn't stay long. They amused themselves by offering each other alcohol with exaggerated shows of politeness and refusing with ever sillier excuses, which Naiz translated for me. The joke occasioned so much hilarity that eventually a gesture of invitation was enough to send everyone into paroxysms of laughter, and some had to retreat to the platform outside to recover.

There were perhaps twenty of us in all, with one chicken to be eaten, and I was disappointed in my faith in tribal equality to find that the men were served first, then the boys and finally the women and girls, who received so little apart from rice it barely seemed worthwhile.

* * *

I woke to a hangover and Harun's precise voice telling me it was time to go. I groaned and turned away from him, which caused the rest of the household, already awake and about their business, to laugh at my bad temper. By the time I got up Iricha was outside in the sun weaving a cane basket, apparently none the worse for the enormous quantity of alcohol he'd consumed the previous evening. His hands and fingers worked by themselves and he hardly glanced at the complicated task while he talked to a friend. I wandered around the village taking photographs. Harun dogged my steps trying to make people pose more formally.

'I am most boring here,' he kept telling me. I had to agree with him although the joke didn't even seem funny to me. He could see no charm in the village or its inhabitants; they meant only money and cheap or free women to him. He harassed me until I lost my temper and told him to go away, we could leave in the afternoon. He protested but I insisted, saying that I'd find my own way back if necessary.

Naiz called to me from her *machang* and I clambered up. She introduced me to her mother and asked if I had any medicine. Patches of skin on the old woman's back had lost feeling and pigmentation, she said. I recoiled in shock, the word 'leprosy' hammering through my hangover, and it took me a moment to recover, to remind myself that only sustained, close contact was infectious. The horror of ages is instilled in the word. I had only aspirins, nothing which would do her any good.

'You should take her to the mission hospital at Chandraghona,' I said, 'that's the only place you'll get medicine for leprosy.'

'Yes, she has leprosy,' Naiz agreed. She indicated that I was to sit down and then sat herself, legs straight out in front of her. 'It is a two or three-day journey to Chandraghona Hospital. Not so much but the army does not allow any tribal to carry more than a week's supply of medicine, for any reason.'

'Why not?'

'They say it is destined for the Shanti Bahini. It's another excuse to harass us. My mother cannot make the journey there and back once a week for the two or three years it takes to cure this disease.' She spoke matter-of-factly, with little bitterness.

'Why don't you complain, or explain the situation to someone?'

'Yes I could.' She paused for a long time. 'The problem is that if you ask anything of the army, complain in any way or try and demand basic human rights then you're branded as a leader, an intellectual, a troublemaker—and then you've had it.'

The old woman was cheerful, despite her affliction. She talked animatedly to her daughter and grinned toothlessly at me.

'My mother says that you look like a good, strong man and if she was younger she'd take you as her husband.'

The woman's eyes half-closed in merriment as her daughter translated and she cackled with laughter. After a few more sallies of this nature she struggled to her feet and hobbled to a large, polished wooden box bound with brass, which was set in a corner of the room. Three cheroots were extracted from within it and lit, then glasses and a bottle of rice spirit. I was in no state to drink and was still uneasily aware of the woman's disease; to drink from a glass which she had no doubt used seemed to be tempting fate. But they wouldn't accept no for an answer.

With great difficulty, for her fingers were already beginning to claw and the nerves to die, the old woman put a carnivorous-looking jungle flower behind my ear. 'Now you look like a Mru,' she said with obvious pleasure.

An hour and too many glasses later we exchanged *namushkars*, and after taking a photograph I climbed unsteadily down. I still have the photograph, mixed up with a few others of Chittagong and of Shiuli, but it's a long time since I looked at any of them; they seem to miss some vital element which lies just beyond the lens's edge and I dislike their insistence on the moment, rather than the continuum.

Harun had packed my few things and was impatient to

leave. As the path turned a corner which would hide the village from our sight I looked back and was suddenly depressed by the anti-climax of departure.

7

THE JOURNEY FROM Cox Bazar to Chittagong was long and tiring because I caught a local bus by mistake. It crawled along, shuddering to a halt every mile or so to pack in more people, goats, sorry-looking chickens, sacks of rice and woven baskets full of plantains. It creaked and groaned like a ship in a storm, the wooden superstructure swaying with the weight on its roof. The driver drove as fast as the pre-war Bedford engine would allow, and made little use of the clutch, which had perhaps worn out, crashing the gears into place by brute force. The area around his seat was decorated with tinsel streamers, fairy lights which flashed when he touched the brakes, quotations from the Koran in Arabic and exhortations not to spit or smoke, not to put heads or hands out of the windows and to watch pockets. Only the last was obeyed.

The conductor collected fares by climbing around the outside of the crowded bus, looking nonchalant and carefree. The wind blew back his thick black hair and ruffled a moustache which would have done justice to a Pathan brigand. The passengers, far from trying to make his task easier, ignored him for as long as they could.

When my neighbour, a solid young man in a scrupulously clean grey check *lungi* who took up two-thirds of the narrow seat, finally deigned to notice the conductor it was only to dispute the fare demanded for himself and six bags of rice. Other passengers quickly joined in the argument and a fight nearly developed between one who supported the conductor's assessment and another who claimed to have a brother working for the same bus company and to have, therefore, an intimate knowledge of the fare structure. The shouting continued until the assistant conductor, who'd been banging on the side of the bus to warn pedestrians and cows of our imminent arrival, forced a way through the crowd and also assailed my neighbour. Attacked on two sides, he grudgingly peeled a note off a wad as thick as his pudgy hand.

I climbed wearily up the four flights to my room, sneaking past the landlord's front door. I disliked both Mr Siddiqui and his wife heartily and did my best to avoid them. While he rarely smiled and liked to discuss the ways of the world in a ponderous manner, she chattered on and screeched with pleasure about nothing.

Somehow I hadn't got around to furnishing my room properly and it had an abandoned air. Books and papers were stacked all over the floor, where insects attacked them and a bright green mould flourished during the monsoon. The balcony served as an inconvenient kitchen, and despite the boards I'd put up wind often blew out my inefficient kerosene stove at a critical juncture, necessitating a messy re-lighting process. For this reason I usually ate out, preferring a restaurant's doubtful hygiene but good food to a poorly cooked meal tainted with kerosene.

A fine yellowish dust coated everything in the room, blown there during my absence by the gusty winter winds. I couldn't face the thought of going out to eat and found the mangos which Shiuli had given me the week before. They were more than ripe and I squeezed one in anticipation of the burst of flavour, like biting into sunlight itself. With a plate on my lap I sliced it twice, either side of the stone. It gave off a rich, sickly-sweet smell. Juice ran down my arms and dribbled from the corners of my mouth as I inverted one lateral slice and bit into pure colour. Hunger quickly overcame the sensual delight and soon half my face was sticky with juice. As I was peeling the last third there was a knock on the door and it opened. I jumped up, spilling what juice had been caught in the plate down my trousers. I swore loudly and then heard Shiuli's laugh. She was on the doorstep, grinning.

'I was passing and saw a light so I came up. I wasn't even sure if it was the right room.'

Mrs Siddiqui peered inquisitively up the stairwell while pretending to clean the newly-painted banisters. She was wearing her hair in hideous, little-girl bunches tied with blue bows. 'You're back Mr Charles,' she screeched. 'Did you have a good time? Do come and have tea with us, we'd love to hear all about it.'

I waved but said nothing and retreated out of sight, beckoning Shiuli to follow. Then I closed and locked the door as quickly as possible. Mrs Siddiqui had an unnerving habit of marching into my room as though it was part of her flat, sitting down and expecting to be entertained.

Shiuli collapsed into fits of laughter, which she tried to stifle with a pillow from my bed. I glimpsed myself in the mirror and saw that my appearance was some cause for laughter. Only a shower and a change of clothes would suffice. My face was streaked with dust and grease from the long bus journey while juice and bits of mango were stuck to me like confetti; some had even managed to get into my hair. I was annoyed that Shiuli should have surprised me looking like a clown.

It was dark by the time I'd showered and changed. Shiuli lay on the bed reading a University exam paper she'd found. It was full of misprints and mistakes which she read out gleefully. Still annoyed with her sense of humour I told her I'd seen them before.

'Oh, Charles, you're so serious. Do you want me to go?'

'No! Please don't. I'm sorry.' I could hardly believe that I'd been rude. She'd come to my room of her own accord, this woman about whom I'd been thinking for days, and I didn't even have the grace to show I was flattered and pleased. I searched around for something positive to say and my energy, fed by her presence, flooded back.

'Will you come and eat with me at the Circuit House?'

I often ate at Chand Kebab, a restaurant which in winter set up tables and chairs on the *maidan*, an expanse of dusty grass in front of the teak-tiled Circuit House.

Mrs Siddiqui was dusting her balcony overlooking the road when we climbed into a rickshaw a few minutes later. The journey took no time but I was overwhelmingly aware of Shiuli's arm touching mine, of the warmth of her skin and of the soft black hairs catching my blond ones.

A small boy ran up to us the moment we arrived. 'Chand

Kebab? Chand Kebab?' he asked breathlessly.

A boy from one of the rival restaurants shouted, 'Paris Kebab? Very much best!' and grinned triumphantly at his mastery of English.

We followed the first boy to a free table where he slapped down two paper napkins, lit the candle and ran off again. Shiuli was the only woman in sight apart from some Europeans sitting together in the Paris Kebab section of the *maidan*. The boy returned quickly, memorised our order and asked if I wanted beer.

'Two beers.'

He spotted more potential customers climbing out of a car and dashed across to them shouting, 'Chand Kebab?'

The boy had served me dozens of times before but still failed to recognise me. I'd even given him a lift home in a rickshaw late one night when I saw him walking exhaustedly past the station. His family lived in a shack built on a stretch of wasteland near the ice factory. Even at that hour the machinery rattled and clanked and belched smoke like an opium addict, while rickshaws emerged from within carrying blocks of steaming ice, like lurid and freakish images from a Fritz Lang film.

'It's a madhouse here,' I commented unnecessarily, thinking that I'd never seen Shiuli looking more attractive. She'd put *kohl* round her eyes and was wearing an indigo sari which shimmered like an early evening sky around the storm cloud of her skin. Her bangles flashed like summer lightning.

The boy came running from the kitchen on the other side of the road, dodging the traffic. He delivered plates of food to another table and crashed two small tea-pots and cups onto ours. We poured ourselves beer from the tea-pots—the restaurant lacked a licence and while the police were no doubt bribed it was as well to observe the decencies.

'To Islam,' Shiuli said as she raised the cup to her lips.

'To Islam.'

'And long may we avoid the *Sharia*.'

'I'll drink to that.'

'I'd leave if the government introduced Islamic law.'

'Very wise, you'd probably be one of its first victims.'

'A dog told Shibli the Sufi that it was being beaten because its master hated to see one better than himself. That's a fair assessment of the *Sharia*, at least in the way it deals with women.'

Shiuli had ordered a salad and it was only when my chicken *tikka* and *tandoori nan* arrived that I remembered she was a vegetarian; a kebab restaurant was not the best place to bring her. I started to apologise but she interrupted.

'I'm not hungry anyway. I ate earlier. I came because of you, not the food.' She smiled, but whether it was at me or at herself, at the solemnity of her tone I couldn't tell.

'And I came because of you. I've been thinking about you all week.'

She raised an eyebrow, 'Even among those lovely tribal women?'

'Especially there. I'm serious, I couldn't get you out of my mind.'

I tore the chicken apart with my fingers and cracked its bones with my teeth, sucking off the heavily spiced flesh with outrageous, exaggerated appreciation.

'I'm probably in a worse mess now than when you turned up at the flat. Such is love.' I uttered the word carefully, looking up at the last moment. 'It leaves you in a worse state than it finds you.'

She loosed a laugh like a kite. 'A changed state, no more no less.'

Two young men in jeans and tee-shirts walked past. One trailed his hand over the back of Shiuli's chair and said something, they both laughed and sat at the next table, talking and glancing at us. The boy went to their table but they told him to go away and pushed him roughly when he said they couldn't stay without ordering a meal. They picked up their chairs and came over, sitting down either side of Shiuli. We stood up quickly and I summoned the boy to pay, but as we walked away they shouted after her in Bengali.

'Is he your boyfriend? Do you fuck? What's the matter with Bengali men? How much do you charge?'

In the rickshaw I pulled the hood up to cover us both, angry and ashamed for exposing her to such insults, but she shook her head. 'I should have known it would happen. It's not your fault.'

She suddenly took my head in her two hands and kissed me ferociously again and again, as though to drive out the memory of what the men had said. 'They're no more than I expect,' she continued, her hands pressed to the sides of my face. 'Things like that happen however and wherever you live, including London. I decided a long time ago that I might as well be as bad as people seemed to assume I was.'

That night we made love on my dusty bed with a passion born of love, isolation and loneliness. Afterwards, as we lay exporing each others' eyes and lips with sensitised fingers, she grew strangely anxious.

'It's hopeless to expect anything normal from this: the city, its people and Islam won't allow it. We'll become crazed and claustrophobic—'

'Don't talk like that before we've even begun.'

'You know there's no equivalent of "to make love" in Bengali. All the acceptable words are metaphors, like *songhom* which means the joining of two rivers.'

'Is it important?'

'There's a kind of intellectual dishonesty about it; we have to dress it up, make it romantic and so avoid facing it as a reality.'

She wouldn't stay the night, saying that Jo and Shomela were expecting her back. After she'd gone, the baby taxi puttering off in a cloud of black exhaust, I felt restless, overwhelmed by the suddenness of what had happened, and although it was late I went out, as though to walk off the effects of some hallucinogen. I followed the rough path around Lal Dighi and caught glimpses of domestic slum life through open doorways. A guttering oil lamp showed me a family of ten, it could have been more, squeezed onto two thin mattresses. A woman standing in a doorway beckoned me furtively and a child peering from behind her skirts pulled her hand down with a whine. I went through Andher Killa where the complaisant domes of Umed Khan's mosque sit like fat men after a meal, and past the British Council Library surrounded by crows' nests of electric wires—a light still burned in the office. In front of the library were two sugarcane crushers, looking like abandoned machines from the industrial revolution, except that nothing is abandoned in a poor country. Beneath them their owners slept on the hard ground, *gumshaws* wound tightly round their heads. Two beggars groaning in a coital embrace on the pavement startled me and I stumbled over broken paving stones, narrowly avoiding a fall into the storm drain; the rich, secret smell of excrement. Way down on the docks a cargo boat was loading and the concussive rattle of an anchor chain being dropped stunned the city, bloated with poverty and disease like a body washed up on the beach at Patenga, half-eaten by crabs and its eyes pecked out by crows; dead to its own horrors. I entered a neon-lit sweet shop and ordered some curd. It had the silky texture of Shiuli's skin, with a tang of salt. The unfiltered ferment of sense impressions, distinguishable only as parts of a whole, each as powerful as the next, suffused me as harshly and completely as hot, raw alcohol.

'The stupid thing is,' she said to me months later, 'that if it wasn't for Islam we wouldn't spend so much time in bed together. It drives us to the very thing it most objects to.'

She was lying propped up on her arms and the moon shone in through the open window, inlaying her dark skin and hair, awry from our lovemaking, with silver.

'Why's that?' I asked sleepily.

'If we could go out more easily without being harassed, to restaurants or to walk around the city, then we wouldn't get so bored here that our thoughts turn naturally to bed.'

*   *   *

I had another key cut and Shiuli was often in my room when I came back from the University, reading or looking up cases in the law books which she brought from work, making a few illegible pencil notes. Otherwise I would listen impatiently for her light, irregular steps on the stairs and go to bed disappointed if she didn't turn up. Sometimes, when she was working hard, I wouldn't see her for three or four days at a time and I'd go down to Armenian Street to leave a note for her. Jo rarely knew where she'd gone and she was often vague about her movements herself, but if he was there I'd sit on the veranda drinking. We invariably ended up talking about her.

One such evening I asked him about finding Shiuli as a baby.

'Shomela found her lying on the veranda, wrapped up tightly in some dirty old rags. Kamrul's father was the guard then and he'd gone out to buy some cigarettes, leaving the street door open. I kept the rags for some reason but they fell apart after a few years. My first reaction was to send the child to a hospital or an orphanage but Shomela insisted that we keep it. She said it was a gift from Allah and that it would be a crime to abandon such a defenceless creature a second time. I was unwilling but Shomela can be pretty forceful when she tries, and anyway I owed her something. She found a wet-nurse and did all the difficult things like that. Apart from naming her Shiuli I took little interest to begin with, but slowly her strange chuckles, smiles and yells affected me.' A smile cracked his rugged face and the blue eyes I'd been so struck by on our first meeting lit up. 'I even began to look forward to finding her here when I got home, to take some pride in her progress, and it became increasingly difficult to imagine life without her. I didn't think of vaccinations and Shomela knew nothing about it, so when we realised that she had polio it was too late. All we could do was try and limit the damage.'

* * *

Two months after our trip to Cox Bazar Mr Siddiqui climbed the stairs, came into my room and sat on the chair looking troubled. '*Salaam-o-Alaikum.*'

'*Alaikum-o-Salaam.*'

After a long silence he raised his dog-like face with its stubbly grey moustache. 'Mr Charles.'

I looked enquiring but said nothing. He shuffled his feet before regaining confidence.

'This is a family building Mr Charles and we consider everyone in it as our family. Like wise parents we are most mindful of the well-being of everyone here.'

'Yes,' I said, suddenly guessing the reason for his visit.

He seemed dissatisfied with the way the discussion was going and tried another tack. 'There are many children in the building Mr Charles and we would not like them to get any wrong ideas. No, most definitely not.' He took courage from this firm assertion, 'There have been complaints that you are harbouring a young woman in your room at all hours, day and night.' He looked at me sternly. 'We abhor such behaviours and we find it contrary to the contract which—'

'You want me to leave Mr Siddiqui?' I was tired of his hectoring tone and pettiness. 'Is that all? I'll go. Thank you Mr Siddiqui.' I held the door open. 'Goodbye Mr Siddiqui.' To my surprise he stood up obediently and shuffled out.

I wasn't even angry, there was no point. I'd stepped outside the boundaries of what was considered decent and he was only doing what he felt was right.

Shiuli's response was gratifyingly immediate. 'Come and live with us. I've already discussed it with Jo. You can have the room at the opposite end of the veranda from mine.'

I ascribe a particular fatefulness to this step. The spores of the future settled firmly with my acceptance of her offer; it was the moment at which it would have been possible to shake them off, perhaps to foresee or forestall the events which were to overshadow us.

I hired a two-wheeled *telegari* and three men from Lal Dighi. They came to the flat: slight men, dark-skinned and muscular, who laughed cheerfully when they saw the light load they'd contracted to push through the streets. We made a strange procession; I led the way in a rickshaw, the *telegari* behind piled high with my chair, a tin trunk filled with books and clothes, and tea-chest. A large Kentia palm in a pot completed the picture, waving its leaves like royalty as we processed.

The men trotted with the *telegari*, one between the shafts like a horse, and two pushing. They sang ribald words to the tune of a popular love song, changing its sentimental lyrics into a complaint at the high prices charged by whores. When I laughed the young rickshaw driver, wearing a white Moslem skull cap, looked disapprovingly at the men, but could hardly keep the grin from his face. Encouraged by my laughter they increased the volume and changed a traditional ballad about a beautiful young woman sitting dreamily in a boat into a lament for her virtue.

In this way we arrived at the house. Neither Shiuli nor Jo was in, but Shomela fussed around us and the men teased her as they carried my things inside, suggesting that she should marry one of them.

She was easily equal to their banter. 'I've been married and I left him—what should I want with types like you who can only sing and drink?'

'Such sweet songs though, mother.'

After they'd gone I asked her whether it was true that she'd left her husband. She looked embarrassed and I thought I'd offended her.

'Two husbands really but I didn't want to tell them that.' Her face wrinkled into a smile. 'I loved one of them although he was no better than that lot—all words. The first was an old *mullah* who already had two wives. My parents arranged it when I was fourteen. I ran away after a month but had his child; a fine boy which died.' She sighed and added, 'It was the will of Allah.'

She took me to the room I'd slept in the first time I'd met Shiuli. It was simply furnished and the old-fashioned four-poster took up a large proportion of the space. The two sets of glass doors and shutters which gave onto the veranda were wide open and the tall whitewashed room was surprisingly cool, unlike my flat—designed for an air-conditioner which I could not afford. Someone, I assumed Shiuli, had hung framed reproductions of Mughal miniatures on the wall and in one corner a bronze cast of Nataraj danced in his circle of fire, spinning effortlessly on one leg to quell Kali's pride.

8

NUMBER 1, ARMENIAN STREET was the background against which Shiuli and I played out our affair. To return to its spacious veranda and cool rooms after a gruelling day in the city or the University was like a release into tenderness. My spirits would lift the moment I came off the crowded street, through the vast wooden doors and into the palm-shaded garden.

There was only one drawback. Jo was often away in the Hill Tracts, but when he returned for a weekend or sometimes longer I would be forced to surrender Shiuli up to his demonstrative love, or rather Shiuli would give herself up to him, for she was not to be possessed by either of us. I consoled myself with the thought that since all his compatriots were either dead or had emigrated he had nothing to identify with, apart from his daughter and whatever memories he could draw from his photographs and books and the building itself. Shiuli tied him to the present and prevented the past coming down like a mist, numbing his senses.

A few months after I moved into their house Jo and I were alone one evening on the veranda playing *Karom*. As was so often the case our conversation turned to Shiuli.

'Just before the Liberation War began, when she was nineteen,' Jo said, pausing to send the red piece cannoning into a pocket, 'I tried to persuade her to go to Nazmah's village home. It's miles out in the country and difficult to get to. In summer it's only accessible by boat. I thought that if, as seemed likely, some kind of civil war started then young, pretty girls were going to be in danger. I was right but Shiuli refused to leave. She carried on as normal, going out, seeing her friends, demonstrating against Pakistani rule and so on.' A black piece skidded into a pocket. 'Five points, sorry about that. I thought it was madness and that she was putting herself unnecessarily at risk but even after that bloody night when the Pakistanis shelled Dhaka University and murdered as many of the intellectuals as they could find, she wouldn't leave.'

'Of course she wouldn't go, she was a member of the Shabohara Party. She was too busy trying to organise resistance.'

Jo looked at me as though I was mad. 'How do you know? I would have known, she would have told me. Shabohara Party?'

'She told me the other day. She joined in her first year at University.'

'But it was banned for its revolutionary ideas.'

'Nazmah says it was the only party which had an idea of what it was doing and a consistent, realistic ideology.'

'Why didn't Shiuli tell me?'

'Perhaps she thought it better that you didn't know.'

'I don't mean at the time, but later. She's not still a member, presumably?'

'No, she'd lost faith in it by '73 and since Siraj Sikdar was arrested and shot while trying to escape, as they say, it didn't have a leader anyway.'

He shook his head. The game was forgotten and he looked hurt, as though he'd discovered Shiuli in some small but emotionally wounding lie, as though the information showed that I was more favoured by her. He may have seen it as a kind of betrayal, a symbol of allegiances which went beyond family ties, further than he could understand.

It was not long after this conversation that I first noticed him becoming strangely withdrawn and subdued. I would hear him wandering aimlessly about his room, picking things up and putting them down again or opening and closing drawers, sighing to himself. It became increasingly difficult to hold a conversation with him and he often didn't listen. He'd emerge from his own world with a senile, 'What? What's that? Hmm?' in response to a question, and then lapse back into silence. I would have put it down to his age except that when Shiuli was present he behaved normally, recovering his mental agility and good humour as though they'd never left him. I was fairly unsympathetic, and I didn't see what I could do, partly because I was as afraid of losing Shiuli as he was. The tension which she engendered between us was never clearly expressed. There was just a slight but constant altering of the frontiers, as between the land and the sea in the forever changing, uncharted waters where the rivers Ganga, Jamuna and Meghna flow into the Bay of Bengal. Alluvium accretes to form a low, sandy *char*, is rounded and smoothed by the action of water and then disappears overnight as one of the inexorable currents which sweep the Bay suddenly and inexplicably changes course.

Shiuli thought I was exaggerating when I described Jo's apparent decline and I had to appeal to Shomela for corroboration. The old woman was curiously unwilling to give a direct answer and instead told a story which began, '*Muktir pore,*' after Freedom. I assumed that she was referring to the period after independence from the British and as it turned out the date was correct; it wasn't until much later that I discovered Mukti had been a woman.

'After Mukti Jo became like he is now. One evening I was starting my shower when I heard a terrific bang from the veranda. I ran through the house with just a sari half-wrapped around me and found Jo holding his army revolver. There was a gecko at his feet, or rather the two halves of a gecko, still wriggling. He'd shot it, you can still see the hole in the plaster. He wouldn't speak, although I shouted at him I was so upset. I hid the revolver then put him to bed. For nearly six months I had to look after him like a child. His friends paid me and gave me money to buy food with.'

This made little sense to me but Shiuli looked thoughtful. The two women ignored my questions, retired to Shomela's room and stayed there for several hours.

'Jo, there's something wrong, what is it?' Shiuli asked him a few nights later when they were alone together on the veranda. I was at my desk but could hear what was said and see Jo, sitting in his customary chair, through a crack between the open door and the wall. He didn't answer but Shiuli went across and stood beside him, then bent down and kissed him on the lips, or so it seemed to me. The delicacy and lightness, the affection held in the kiss made me absurdly jealous. His arms came around her shoulders and he held her close, one hand stroking her loose hair. He said something in a low voice which I didn't catch, but I was beginning to feel like a voyeur and I shifted my chair so that I couldn't see them.

From that time on Jo spent more time in our company and he often came with us in the evenings to Nazmah's place, to see a film or to eat in one of the many Chinese restaurants.

I once asked Shiuli whether they'd ever been lovers. We were crossing the Karnaphuli river in a sampan and the silence was broken only by the creaking of the oars in their rope rowlocks and the splash of water around the bow. Suspended between air and water the place seemed neutral enough to ask such an indiscreet question, or perhaps it was that no question, no answer seemed impossible in such surroundings, with the open, dry blue above us and the muddy water beneath, flowing determinedly towards the Bay with its load of silt to build more impermanent islets and *chars*. Petty human sensitivities appeared absurd. I would have been surprised if she'd said yes, but asked from a need to know what her reaction would be rather than in a real spirit of enquiry. It was part of the imperative to construct a true picture of her, as though in preparation for some disaster.

'Your questions are like those of a child sometimes; only an innocent or a fool could be so ingenuous. The answer's no.'

* * *

One evening Jo returned from the Hill Tracts and went straight to his room without saying a word as he passed us on the veranda. He emerged some two hours later looking terrible.

'We were on our way home but still in the Hill Tracts,' he explained, 'near to a place called Panchari, when Tarith suddenly swung the Landcruiser off the main road and down a narrow track. Creepers and branches scraped the sides. He ignored my demands to return to the road, affecting not to hear, even when I threatened him with dismissal.' He gulped some of the whisky I'd poured for him. 'The track became more and more difficult and at one point we were in danger of getting stuck completely. You can't imagine how thick the jungle is there, it's impossible to see beyond the first yard and without a machete it's impenetrable. Perfect place for a kidnap, I thought. Finally a tree trunk blocked the path and we were forced to stop. Tarith got out and climbed over the trunk, beckoning me to follow. He still said nothing and didn't even smile as he usually does when I'm angry. By this time I was intrigued so I followed, a little warily. I thought he was going to show me an illegal elephant *kheda* or something of that kind. After about twenty minutes we came to a big clearing on the brow of a hill; the area had been burnt, nothing remained but a few bamboos standing vertically out of the ground. Tarith stopped and looked at me.

'"This is my family's village," he said. "Three days ago the army burnt it down. Some escaped. This is what your road is doing for us tribals."

'He brushed past me and began to walk back towards the car. I stared around and realised that the bamboos had been supports for *machangs*. By one group I found a broken clay pot, next to it were some small, charred bones. I didn't look any further.'

His voice trailed away and it was hard to catch the next few words. 'Though I'm sure they were the bones of a piglet.'

The three of us sat in the half-darkness looking out over the grey-blues of the garden. Shomela's goat bleated in an unconvinced way and began to climb the veranda steps, nibbling at the roses which grew there.

'I went back to the car,' Jo continued, 'and found Tarith already reversing up the path. He wouldn't speak until we'd nearly reached Chittagong. Then the worst part began. Usually we talk to each other in Bengali but this time he spoke in English, slowly and carefully, as though to distance himself from what he was saying. He didn't spare me the details but, briefly: Only two boys escaped because they were tending pigs in the jungle. The women were raped repeatedly and taken away. The men were killed. Forty-three people in all. Tarith said, "Your road," as though it was my personal road, as though I'm responsible for what the army does.'

'But Jo, it's true. You must know that,' Shiuli said gently.

'No I don't know that. The road is for the tribals. It's supposed to make life easier for them. You know how inaccessible most of the district is.'

'Yes, and you know how the tribals have always been exploited and used by us Bengalis. You know why the British banned Bengali businessmen from the area. You know that half the Chakma's total agricultural land was flooded by the Kaptai dam, and that hardly any of them received any compensation. You know there's a war going on. You know all that, or you should, yet still you're prepared to believe that this time the government—Bengalis, remember—wants to build roads for the good of the tribal people.'

I'd never heard Shiuli so angry with her father before.

'They've got to come into the twentieth century sometime. Roads will help them reach markets and sell their produce.'

'You don't believe that. What do you think the Shanti Bahini are fighting for? Because they don't want to come into the twentieth century or because they don't want all their land and forest to be stolen by Bengalis?'

The goat came up a step and nibbled at a geranium.

'Why do you say this now?' I asked. 'Jo's had the job for over a year and you've never mentioned it before.'

'Because I hadn't thought about it much. But Jo's story makes it obvious. Of course the roads are more useful to the army than anyone else. How wide are they?'

'Thirty-two feet,' he replied promptly.

'Thirty-two feet! They're supposed to be for a few tribals walking barefoot with some fruit and veg and you're building thirty-two foot-wide metalled roads. Wide enough to take tanks or armoured cars. Now we can do to the tribals what the Pakistanis tried to do to us, for the same reasons. We can wipe them out without any trouble—we've been trying for long enough.'

'How was I to know?' Jo asked no one in particular. '"Your road", Tarith blames me.'

I'd like to think that I felt sympathetic towards Jo, for I too had suffered from Shiuli's anger, but foolishly taking it as a symbol of my ascendancy in her affections I exulted. In fact it was the beginning of what I later perceived as my own, not Jo's defeat.

The silence of the walled garden enfolded us until an imam began the call to prayer. The call was taken up by others near and far until the sky seemed to reverberate with the noise. I'd heard it hundreds of times before, but it was an eerie and alien sound that night.

Shortly after this experience Jo seemed to snap out of the dejection which I'd found so wearying. I asked Shiuli if she thought he'd recovered.

'He does seem more like he used to be; happier and louder, even fiercer.'

'Prepared to fight again?' At the time I imagined that Shiuli's closer attendance had had the desired effect.

* * *

Living with Shiuli I began to feel the different pulses of the city. She was at home anywhere in the sprawling conglomeration of miserable *bustees*, the decaying, crowded flats or the grand houses owned by missionary societies, Grindlays Bank, the Ispahanis and other wealthy business families (including Nazmah's), which topped each conical hill. Houses lifted out of the infected swamps and stews. Mushtaque once told me that London, in comparison with Chittagong, was dirty and it was a long time before I realised that he was blind to Chittagong's filth and horrors, for he never walked the streets, never had to brush shoulders with the poor in the Underground or a bus queue and was as astonishingly ignorant of its realities as he might have been of Echmiadzin.

We made many expeditions into the back streets and noisome alleys of the city and were sometimes able to persuade Nazmah to accompany us, but she disliked crowds and her extravagant gestures and loud voice always attracted attention. We were frequently surrounded by the curious, and though we could ignore the occasional insult it was this which reduced our enthusiasm for walking the city and finding old palaces, temples or mosques hidden by the haphazard jungle of the new. Nazmah knew something about every building of interest and with her passionate expositions was able to renew the rotting brickwork for us, to remould the plaster ceilings and to conjure up the ghosts of the nawabs, the Moslem saints and British Collectors which haunted such ruins. She hated the destruction of the old buildings and had spent enormous sums photographing whatever remained of them.

'They're part of our historical patrimony. People shouldn't be allowed to forget the importance of the past. Things are forgotten so quickly here. All the promises made in '71 were broken within four years and the political scum was allowed to rise to the surface again. If we had a better historical sense these things might not happen so easily,' she would argue.

Jo laughed at such ideas. To reason from the concrete back to the abstract didn't make much sense to his practical mind or his training as an engineer. The worst arguments between him and Nazmah revolved around the fate of the Armenian Church, for while Jo thought it should be allowed to fall down 'in peace', Nazmah believed wholeheartedly in preservation.

'If you're so much against conservation why do you keep that brick from Pandita Vihara?' Shiuli demanded.

'I need a paperweight.'

'Jo—'

'Yes, all right, I'll be serious.' He fetched the little terracotta brick from his desk and gave it to Nazmah, who was horrified.

'How did you get this?'

'During the War the Cantonment was extended and the contractors bulldozed a large proportion of what was left of the Vihara. I thought that if they were going to destroy it I might as well take a bit. This was the prettiest I could find.'

'Preserve it in other words,' Nazmah said.

'If you like, but I think there's a difference between a building falling down naturally, being overgrown and softening in the damp, to being knocked down by machines. One is an inevitable process, the other wilful. I wouldn't have touched it if the contractors hadn't been there. By the time they were stopped it seemed foolish to go and put it back.'

Nazmah peered closely at the thousand-year-old bas-relief, the image still sharply defined and as alive as the day it had been fired. 'She's beautiful.'

'She does dance well, doesn't she? She looks as though she might jump off the stone at any moment.'

* * *

Once a week Shiuli and two colleagues gave free legal advice in one of the *bustees*, spending the day among the carved, wide-eyed faces of the consumptives and permanently malnourished, the open drains and ramshackle houses made of tin, cardboard and pieces of sacking. I accompanied her twice but it made me uncomfortable to listen to their stories of abandonment and exploitation, to be confronted by underprivilege on such a scale, and to know that I was doing nothing about it. Yet these weren't the poorest, for they had a roof at least. Beneath them, even exploited by them, were the rag and paper-pickers, the bottle and tin can-recoverers, the orphans: the absolutely destitute in the fine grading of poverty.

One girl I had particular reason to remember. She was about seventeen, had two small children and had been abandoned by her husband. Her gaunt face and hard eyes were devoid of all self-pity as she told Shiuli how her employer forced his sexual attentions on her. She recounted the facts without emotion, knowing it to be a common complaint among servants, almost an accepted part of their duties. Shiuli outlined the difficulties of bringing charges, the bias of the police and courts and explained that they could file a case but that it would be difficult to win as the man would surely bribe the judge.

'I know all that,' the girl interrupted, 'and I can't afford to lose the job, that's why I came to you; I hoped there might be some other way out.' She looked directly at Shiuli as she spoke, taking in her long hair, unfaded cotton sari and bangles chinking like promises of money on her dark wrist.

The girl's name was Fatima and she stared at Shiuli without suspicion or jealousy, as far as I could tell, but like everyone who came for advice her manner suggested that she had no expectations and that life held no more terrors for her—she'd already lived ten lives in her few years.

Encounters such as this could depress Shiuli unutterably, for there was no simple answer and little she could do in such circumstances. She'd come home with the spirit knocked out of her and frequently send Kamrul out to buy ganja, take down a book of poetry from one of the glassed-in shelves and immerse herself in Yeats or Nazrul Islam, Shelley or Shamsur Rahman.

'It's the only way I can read poetry now. Without ganja I can't concentrate or relax enough. There are too many other things buzzing around in my head.'

Sinking into the cushions of the sofa she'd stretch herself out, ignoring everything around her as though the only bearable reality lay in poetic imagery. I found that ganja made her unapproachable and distant, as though her own existence was the only one she was certain of.

Once Shiuli stayed at home for two days, sitting under the fan in the main room.

'Is revolution really the only answer?' she asked me listlessly. 'All that killing and blood to try and make the place a little fairer, with no certainty of success.'

I had no answer but asked what had induced this depression.

'Oh nothing really, nothing unusual anyway. You remember the girl Fatima who was always being raped by her employer? She went to the police station to file a case against him without telling me first, was locked up and raped by the police for three days.' She flicked a *Karom* piece across the chalked board and it ricocheted around before disappearing into a pocket. 'When she was released, she went back to her job and was told she'd been fired for not turning up. The most sickening aspect of the whole thing is that none of it surprises or even shakes her very much. That, to her, is what life is like. It's no less than she expects.' Another *Karom* piece cracked across the board.

I tried to warn her of the dangers inherent in this work in the *bustees*. She knew them, of course, knew that ultimately it would bring her into uncompromising conflict with the authorities.

'I know what I'm doing.' She was sitting naked in the middle of my bed, with her legs curled up under her. 'I'm careful not to challenge anyone until I'm sure of my ground, and I'm perfectly aware that to bring a case against the police is difficult.'

'And dangerous.'

She lay down, her withered leg pressed against mine. Its skin surface trembled slightly, like the batting of her eyelashes on my cheek after we'd made love. It was as though there was something soft and vulnerable fluttering inside the twisted limb, wanting freedom and escape.

'It's one of the reasons I've decided to take up human rights issues on a big scale. At the moment we're just scratching the surface, providing palliatives. We'll start off with a few small cases: *bustee* dwellers whose houses have been bulldozed by the government. Perhaps that's a big case. Prostitutes who've been imprisoned without trial then, or destitutes picked off the streets and held in camps. Have you ever seen one of those places? They remind me of photos of concentration camps; the same fatalistic expressions, as though they've forgotten who they were.'

Such was my worry about Shiuli antagonising the army and government that I tried to make Nazmah help me dissuade her from becoming more involved than she already was in what I termed marginal activities.

Nazmah was incredulous. 'You're joking! Don't you know her better than that yet? There's no chance of persuading her to stop, none at all; she may because she decides to, but not because we ask her.'

'I suppose so.'

'I know so. When Shiuli was about sixteen she wanted to

become a badminton champion. She worked and worked to overcome the handicap of her leg and developed a demon return but obviously she wasn't quick enough about the court—'

'She still beats me—'

'Yes, she even fought her way into the national school championships but was knocked out early on. The point is that the idea itself was unrealistic, however good she became she'd never have been able to compete with someone who was competent and had two good legs. But there was no point in telling her that.'

The *bustee* work could also give her highs. If the day had gone well she'd return full of energy and drag Jo and myself out into the bazar to stroll through the early evening crowds, or to a newly opened sweet shop. The savour of sweet names: *kalojam*, *roshmalai*, *gulabjamun*, as thick and sensual as the sweets themselves. We would get drunk on sugar, like the flies which infested such places, while Shiuli talked, often brilliantly it seemed to me. She might take boats as her theme, and arguing that they represented the true culture of Bangladesh she'd rail against contrived Mughal sophistication in poetry and music.

'It's a vertically structured culture of exclusion. Real Bengali culture lies in the verbal, historical traditions of the people who live and work on boats, and with village women who, shut out from male-centred cultural and religious concepts, retain ancient rites, practices and beliefs from before the Buddha.'

I usually found myself agreeing with her but although Jo argued forcefully against such ideas he would only dispute them with her, ignoring whatever I said.

* * *

We went to the Club infrequently, once to see the film *Heat and Dust* (Jo stood up with an oath after ten minutes and left, muttering, 'God save me from bloody romantic India') and once to hear the sitar player Nikhil Banerji. The Club's dance hall, with its pillars and sprung floor, was decorated with sprays of bougainvillaea for the occasion and cushions were laid out for the audience to sit on. The room was packed and we squeezed in at the back as the virtuoso came onto the raised platform at one end of the room, his gold-embroidered *kurta* scattering light like water droplets. People stirred and applauded then continued to converse in low voices while he tuned his instrument.

The sitar's notes played around the rapid patter of a *tabla* as effortlessly as a cat plays with a bird. Harmonies caught up with and flowed over one another like water over rocks, swirling and eddying, breaking into ripples and plunging into deep, slow pools: music as the interpretation of feeling, the construction of a mood. Almost unnoticeably the *raag* built into a crescendo of sound. It was like watching the birth of a world; silver light before the first dawn, an endless horizon and music providing the details—shadows of birds and butterflies, fish in the rivers and sticky fruit on the trees, waiting to be plucked.

As usual the audience talked throughout the performance; to most of them being seen there was more important than the music itself.

When the *raag* ended I was brought to earth by an awareness of my cramped limbs and by Jo stretching beside me. We wandered outside and stopped on the edge of the veranda.

'Sometimes this music angers and saddens me,' Shiuli said thoughtfully, leaning on the balustrade and looking across the city. 'It's music based on the idea of immutability. It's not been allowed to change in four or five hundred years. The whole point is to learn the tradition from a master, a *Poddosri*, the pure form, just as he learnt it from a *Poddosri* who in turn. . . . A musical tradition passed down from teacher to student through centuries with no room for innovation. It's so rooted in conservatism. Ravi Shankar tried to move it along an inch and people reviled him instead of loving him for trying. All they could say was that he'd corrupted the pure tradition and was therefore bad. They didn't even listen to him.'

She was always disconcerting me like this. My ideas were as subject to change under her influence as some volatile liquid exposed to oxygen. Perhaps I surprised her as well, but if so I did it unknowingly, whereas her mental ambushes were planned and invariably provoked me into re-thinking long-held opinions and ideas.

I leant over the balustrade next to her and looked up; clouds were icing up the stars. 'But it's three-quarters improvisation—'

'Improvisation within narrow, strictly defined boundaries, that's what I'm complaining about.'

I sighed involuntarily but Jo voiced my thought. 'When will you stop wanting to change the world, Shiuli?'

'When I'm cured of my limp and no one catches polio any more,' she replied harshly.

'But it doesn't change. All you do is shift things around a little.'

'Share out the good and bad a bit more equitably in other words, break up concentrations of evil—'

'I mean that you don't reduce the amount of evil in the world.'

'And I mean that I didn't say anything about doing that. Wanting to change the world is different to believing you have an evangelical mission to make it good. Goodness is a false god.'

The concert began again but we stayed where we were. The sitar's soaring harmonies were quickly joined by a purl of notes on the *tabla*, the player's fingers, thumbs and the base of his hands all producing distinct sounds, leaping over the sitar's streams and pools. The rhythm grew faster and the instrumentalists seemed to compete to contain each other in cages of gold and silver filigree. The music soared outwards and upwards into the void.

For my part there was nothing more wonderful than to be listening to Nikhil Banerji, to be looking at the frosted milky way and to be standing beside Shiuli.

* * *

Arrest finally put paid to our enjoyment of the city itself. It was early afternoon and we were walking towards Armenian Street from the ferry *ghat* through Abhoy Mitra and Alkaran roads. The smell of frying sweets and old jute mixed strangely with that of the river. The city seemed to take short, shuddering breaths under the weight of the damp heat, its walls and minarets deliquescing like sugar back into the vast alluvial delta system.

Two policemen blocked our way in the narrow street. Deep in conversation, we started to go around them but they put their batons out to prevent us. They both had narrow, hatchet-like faces and pencil-thin moustaches. One asked Shiuli where she was going, to which she replied that it was none of his business. This response angered them and the taller of the two turned to me. 'What's your name? Where are you taking this woman?'

Before I could reply Shiuli repeated that unless they suspected us of committing a crime they had no right to detain us.

'We are arresting you on a charge of prostitution,' one of them said as though suddenly inspired.

'Both of you,' the other added, tapping me lightly on the arm with his baton and grinning.

I made some facetious remark about male prostitution but no one understood except Shiuli, who muttered, 'Idiot.'

It all seemed a bit of a joke, except that by this time a crowd had begun to gather, those at the back asking those at the front what was happening. I heard the word *maal*, 'whore', being passed back like a precious gift. We stood there for a few minutes arguing, Shiuli at her magnificent, angry best. Traffic came to a standstill, blocked by the ever-increasing crowd. It was only when a few wary shopkeepers pulled down their metal shutters, anticipating a riot, that I realised the situation was serious. People were being pushed up against us and the two policemen had begun to look uneasy, to threaten the crowd with their batons.

'You must come with us,' the smaller of the two said, wiping the sweat from his unshaven chin. We had little option by that time and we followed them thankfully as they forced a way through the packed, jostling mass of male bodies.

'Prostitution isn't an arrestable offence,' Shiuli told me, with no apparent concern. 'I'll make these two clowns sorry they ever set eyes on us—'

A hand shot out and squeezed her bottom through the thin cotton sari. She turned and slapped the offender so hard that he fell back into the crowd.

The crowd was immediately silent at this unexpected, exciting turn of events. The silence lasted less than five seconds, but the scene is frozen in my memory: a sea of dark, expectant faces turned towards Shiuli and the man, who was rubbing his cheek, surprise and anger competing for supremacy on his handsome face; the two policemen looking back over their shoulders in alarm, ready to flee should the crowd turn nasty; and a traffic-jam of rickshaws, wheels locked and colourful as butterflies, stretching down the street.

'If I'm a tart I'm too expensive for you to even touch, so keep your greedy hands to yourself,' Shiuli said loudly, grim-faced.

The tension evaporated as the joke was repeated and the whole mob began to laugh. Even the man who'd been slapped smiled wrily, acknowledging defeat. They dispersed, still laughing, although a few of the more determined followed us to the doors of the police station. Once there Shiuli gave her fury free rein, throwing their laughable attempts to question or charge us back in their faces and demanding a written apology. Soon the whole station was in an uproar.

The argument proceeded in true comic style with neither side listening to the other, until by sheer force of personality Shiuli convinced the officer that she was a barrister, not a prostitute. He then announced that we couldn't be released without authorisation from someone higher up the chain of command. We were passed upwards in this way two or three times and each time the argument had to be gone through again.

'If you're a barrister what are you doing with this foreigner?'

Shiuli was completely fed up by this time. 'He's a judge from London and has come to see how justice works in this country. I'm showing him around.'

'He's very young to be a judge.'

'Yes, but he's very clever and he's not getting a good impression.'

I thought she'd overstepped the mark but put on my most solemn Judge Jeffrey's look and this seemed to have some impact, for soon afterwards we were given tea and left alone. However, the next officer to question us evinced more interest in the work of a judge in Britain than in the reasons for our arrest. It was proof that we'd won but I was hard put to make up convincing answers and it was three hours before we were released, without a written apology.

9

TIRING OF THE city we turned our backs on its provincialism and spent most of our spare time exploring the countryside, where only the poor receive rough treatment, or with Boddhipal.

There were only five monks, all tribals from the Hill Tracts, in the monastery over which Shiuli's friend, Boddhipal, presided. We used to talk for hours in his cell-like room which contained little other than a plain wooden bed, a worm-eaten table and a single chair. A cheap bazar poster Sellotaped to the wall depicted an emaciated Buddha seated beneath a bodhi tree, one hand touching the ground. Demons, monsters and seductive women filled the air around him. Inscriptions in English and Bengali said, 'The Boddhisattva seeks Enlightenment and is assaulted by the hosts of Mara, the Evil One.'

'The Buddha-to-be was thirty-five,' Boddhipal explained, 'when he attained Enlightenment. It happened at a small place called Bodh Gaya in Bihar. Every Buddhist nation has a temple there now. The most beautiful is the Japanese one, it floats above the plain and seems to be built of space and light. We of course, not being a nation, have no temple.'

On the table in front of his window was a glass which always contained a flower, an hibiscus, gardenia, or sometimes a rare, thick-petalled magnolia. His books, in dusty piles under the bed, were mainly religious texts in Pali but included an Indian edition of Shelley's poems which I gave him.

When he sat on his bed, straight-backed and animated, he filled the austere room with light and life. His feminine air, gentle and loving quite apart from his physical beauty, made me think that he'd never had to surround himself with the barriers and defences with which men often define themselves. He was a true child of the forest; his quietness and simplicity forced me to notice the weight of my pretentions and desires. It was not only a spiritual quality. He moved silently, slipping in and out of rooms with grace and a lithe economy of movement, his orange robe rippling like the pelt of a great cat over its bunched muscles.

His life was strictly regulated but he allowed himself the indulgence of a small Burmese cheroot once in a while, taking a childish delight in them. He lit them with an ancient petrol lighter, and to watch him use this contraption was to hold one's breath in anticipation of calamity as blue flames ran around the top and flashed down the sides, sometimes burning his fingers. He was none the less proud of it and I teased him about his attachment to this possession. He had countered the charge by offering it to me as a gift, one which I refused on the grounds that without guaranteed divine protection I wouldn't dare operate it.

Shiuli thought of him as a free spirit, a will-o'-the-wisp and said that his ideas 'danced in the darkness'.

'He's not unwilling to make categorical statements, he doesn't talk in riddles.'

'That's not what I meant. It's more that what he says has a finished quality. It's simple without being naïve and is his own. If you or I expressed the same ideas the words would have to be different.'

'As he says, "Each of us must arrive at our own truth and our own way of expressing it."'

When he, his fellow monks and the children were in their simple temple, little more than a room with a statue of Buddha at one end, it was impossible not to be affected by the unhurried gestures of devotion made in the flickering light of plain clay oil lamps.

Early on in our friendship I asked him why he didn't live at the main monastery in Chittagong. We were working in the school's vegetable patch where I often helped him in the evenings, enjoying the feel of damp soil between my toes and the exercise. He was digging so slowly that I'd completed two rows to his one.

'Because I feel it necessary to do more than meditate and pray. At Nandankanan monastery there is only religion and, of course, a hair relic of the Buddha.' He smiled sadly before bending to his work again. 'Also most of the monks are Bengalis, good people in their way, but they do not understand what it is to be in a racial minority. Here, with our twenty-eight boys from Buddhist families, we are not just parasitic monks.' He paused. 'The expression isn't mine,' he said before continuing: 'I want to give back more than religious words and symbols. Education is a gift which few in Bangladesh receive. If we manage to educate these boys properly—' He dropped the hand plough with a cry and extracted a worm from the loose soil, deliberately placing it in a safe place where it wouldn't run the risk of being chopped in half. I might have laughed at such a thing once, but it was done with such intent purposefulness that I hardly smiled.

'You feel the necessity of achieving something?'

'You try to trap me. Achieve something in the sense of achieving for others. It is not for myself that I teach but for the boys.'

It was about the same time as our arrest that we discovered the extent of Boddhipal's conflict. We found him hunched at the table which served him as a desk when we arrived, and he greeted us with less than his usual enthusiasm.

'I received news from a village called Gorosthan,' he said when we asked how he was. 'Two days ago the army smashed the image of Lord Buddha in our temple there, slaughtered a cow inside and broke the arms of Venerable Jyotipal Bhikkhu. He is seventy-eight years of age, a humble old man with no thoughts other than to serve the Buddhist faith and his people. He is my teacher and has been for thirty years. Why should the army do such things? It's as though they want our young men to take to the jungle and fight.'

His normally clear face creased into a frown and he glanced at an old and dog-eared copy of *Time* lying face up on his bed. The cover showed Bobby Kennedy beneath the headline, 'Civil Rights: The Moral Crisis', and a quotation: 'It is time to act in all of our daily lives.'

'How terrible, Boddhipal. Is there anything we can do?'

He looked up and smiled sadly at Shiuli. 'No, there is nothing we can do but talk about it.'

Shiuli and I were silent in the face of his despair. Only by doing violence to himself, to his gentle instinct, by ripping the sacred saffron robe from his back and exchanging it for a gun, could he hope to stem the destruction of his tribal family. The concept was unthinkable to one so immersed in *ahisma*.

'I've been trying to meditate all day but I'm unable to concentrate. I wanted to reach an understanding of my role in all this, of how to be of use to my people but the idea of blood defiling an image of Lord Buddha kept interfering. Blood!'

To hear Boddihipal talk in this way was like finding a previously healthy friend palsied and incontinent. I'd always assumed that meditation came naturally and easily to him under any circumstances, but then my experience was limited. Shiuli did, and I tried to, meditate every morning on the wide, cool veranda, much to Shomela's stifled amusement. Shiuli remained far in advance of me, for she had both a greater interest and a clear rationale.

'The two perceived options in Bangladesh open to those who can do more than work and starve are excessive mysticism and arid intellectualism. Most of us opt for the latter—it seems to suit our temperament. Both are ways of dealing with the pain and misery around us. The Occidental way was to work hard and to build walls—look at this place.' She gestured across the garden at the massive walls and gateway. 'Or to run away, to leave. Meditation is another way of dealing with it, a way which encourages one to face the inevitable challenge.'

My progress in meditation was hindered by being unable to take it seriously. All religious ideas seemed equally good to me, equally likely to achieve whatever ends they desired. Nor could I release myself from an awareness of Shiuli's physical presence, of the kisses we'd stolen perhaps only a few minutes earlier. My attention would stray back to my room, with the early morning light splayed through the Venetian shutters and Shiuli divesting herself of sleep with the slow sensuality of an excoriating serpent. I knew that the whole point was not to allow the attention to wander, but enjoyed these illicit thoughts too much to want to give them up. When Boddhipal gave us instruction in meditation I listened without taking much in, for it was Boddhipal the man who fascinated and entranced me.

Shiuli recovered first; she fiddled with Boddhipal's kerosene stove until it lit and put some water on to boil. Her hands shook, so disconcerted was she to find him in this state.

Through the open door of his room we could see boys playing in the pond, leaping off the bank into the dark green water and splashing each other. Their shouts and laughter floated over to us and filtered through a double line of coconut palms whose leaves hung down lifelessly, their sharp edges blurred by the glare off the water, much as physical reality lost its precision in our conversations with Boddhipal.

'We are not a violent people. We never have been, but what can we do against a government and an army which wants to exterminate us?' He paused. 'It is a question. I need an answer for myself and for all of us who remain.'

What could we have said? It was useless. Could we have said 'Fight!' and then been able to bear his look of hurt and humiliation? It was perhaps what he wanted to hear.

I sat on his bed and picked up the magazine he'd glanced at earlier. It fell open at the photograph of Quang Duc sitting in the lotus position in his monk's robes, as inanimate as a stone statue of the Buddha. Ragged petrol flames leapt six feet into the air above him, consuming his robe, hair and flesh. I read:

> The automobile at the head of the procession of saffron-robed Buddhist monks in Saigon suddenly choked to a stop at an intersection. The occupants of the car lifted its hood as chanting priests began forming a circle seven or eight deep around the vehicle. Prayer beads clutched in his hand, a phlegmatic, 73-year-old monk named Thich Quang Duc sat down cross-legged on the asphalt in the center of the circle. From under the auto's hood, a monk took a canister of gasoline and poured it over the old priest. An expression

of serenity on his wizened face, Quang Duc suddenly struck a match. As flames engulfed his body he made not a single cry nor moved a muscle.

Boddhipal saw what I was reading. 'I could not do it, Charles, even if I wanted to. It would be too difficult for me. I'm sorry, this is not the way to treat friends. Shiuli, please, let me make the tea. There is lemon here also. Even if I wanted to, who would take any notice?' He sliced a lemon. 'What is happening to my land and people is a local issue. No one is interested in Bangladesh, whereas Vietnam was already an issue in '63 and after this affair the Americans put pressure on President Diem to lift restrictions on Buddhists. They knew that his prejudice was driving the peasants further into the hands of the Viet Cong.'

'Don't you ever think of moving to Calcutta or Agartala?' I asked.

He stopped slicing lemons and the knife, held delicately in his left hand, hovered in mid-air.

'I think of it often. I feel that I'm hitting my head on a wall here. Is that the expression? But it would be a defeat to go. Though many of my people and other Bhikkhus have been driven to India I still believe that something can be achieved. I will leave when I stop believing.'

'There's a tribal boy, a Chakma in my first-year class at the University. He's bright enough but the other students laugh at his English because he mispronounces different words to them. They seem to regard him as a kind of fool, a jester who's tolerated because he makes everyone else feel superior.'

'That's the general attitude of Bengalis to us. We are primitive jungle folk with no culture and no wisdom, only fit to be slaughtered.'

'You know who owns most of the timber businesses in the Hill Tracts now?' Shiuli asked me.

'No.'

'High-ranking army officers.'

'How's that?'

'The businesses used to be owned by rich tribals, but the army arrests them then refuses to release them until they've signed away ownership. It's too easy.'

Boddhipal nodded and poured tea into pale green, porcelain bowls. 'A Japanese visitor gave me these bowls last week, he also promised some money for the school. The Japanese like the idea of supporting Buddhist schools, as the Saudis like to support mosques and *madrasas*.' He paused to stir his tea. 'They're building a mosque in Rangamati at the moment, in our heartland. Perhaps if we all converted to Islam we'd stand a chance of survival.'

It was the bitterest remark I ever heard him make.

Part Three

10

I DROVE OVER a rag in the middle of the road. There was a noise like a tyre bursting and I stopped to investigate. The rag was a child; I'd driven over its skull. Blood was spattered up the white paint. People began to run across the paddy fields towards me, picking up weapons as they came. Sweating, I climbed back into Jo's Landcruiser and tried to turn it on the narrow road. I was too slow. A mob of angry men and women barred the way and began to beat the bonnet with their sticks; chips of paint flew off. They shouted and leered in at me. The windscreen was shattered by a brick and I felt blood trickle from a cut on my forehead. I twisted in the seat and woke. A mynah bird chattered incessantly in the mango tree beyond the shutters of my room. Its harsh, metallic rattle had a vicious ring to it.

It was early, six-thirty, but my room was already stifling, sweat ran across my forehead and the mattress was damp. The fan was motionless, no electricity again. My first thought was of Jo as I'd seen him the previous day in the army morgue. The corpse was alien to the man but it was so powerful an image that it overrode other memories. His chin had had a slight growth of stubble, patched white in places, and for some reason it seemed particularly macabre that some part of the body should continue to function after death. I tried to recall the exact tenor of his voice but it became confused with other voices and with the disquieting racket of the mynah.

I didn't want to get up or to face whatever the day would bring, but it was too hot to lie there. Shomela was grinding spices in the kitchen, the stones sounding like distant thunder, and the smell of garlic, turmeric and chilli drifted into the room as I padded across the cracked old tiles to the bathroom. Shomela had been with Jo for nearly forty years whereas I'd only known him eighteen months. My depression at his unexpected death could hardly be as deep as hers, yet she was working, as always ensuring that the household could be fed.

The shower washed off the night's sweat and cleared my head of its morbid dream. I went back over my conversations with Major Rahman. His explanation of the accident had been simple enough but two questions had apparently unnerved him. It was as though he'd had to search for answers when I'd asked where the Landcruiser was, and again when I asked whether he'd been there. *This morning*, he'd said, and it had sounded like a denial of guilt. His manner had been sympathetic, but why had he been so open about his dislike of the war in the Hill Tracts? *It's a hateful war ... I'd get out if I could.* Had he wanted to find out my opinion? There was no reason. Perhaps he'd found the process difficult and had to talk about something, but I couldn't shake off the impression that he'd been appraising me.

A cockroach peered out from a crack in the wall. I kicked water at it and it retreated hurriedly. Water. It had only started to rain yesterday, yet Jo had skidded on the muddy road the night before. Was that what Rahman had said? I racked my brains to no effect, then pushed the thought aside. What about Tarith, Jo's driver? I'd forgotten to ask and Rahman hadn't mentioned him. Perhaps he'd not been there.

I dried and went into the kitchen where Shomela was squatting on the floor, grinding stones in front of her. She said, 'Good morning,' in English, as she did every morning. I poured myself some coffee and went onto the veranda.

Shiuli was already there. The orange early morning light filtered through the leaves of the ancient hibiscus bushes, so ravaged by goats that they'd become ugly, tortured stems topped by a knot of leaves and bright scarlet flowers. The air was still and the veranda steps dry, despite the evening's downpour. The poor woman who'd arrived in the rain sat on the steps in the sun, breast-feeding her baby. I'd forgotten her; she must have spent a miserable, lonely night. I asked her if she'd eaten and she replied that she'd slept in Shomela's room and had been fed by her earlier.

'We should go to the Cantonment today to pick up his

things,' I said to Shiuli, 'and we could ask about Tarith. I forgot about him yesterday.'

She didn't respond. She was hunched forward on the edge of her chair and held her coffee cupped in two hands as though to warm them, although beads of sweat glistened on her forehead and upper lip.

I left her to herself and for some reason my thoughts shifted back to an insignificant event which had occurred two days earlier. I'd been about to leave for the University when Shiuli had come up close to me. I could smell the freshness of her body and of her raven hair, still damp from her morning shower. I touched her bare arm under the sari and she pressed up closed.

'Let's make love,' she said.

'I can't. I've got a lecture first thing.'

'Miss it.'

I pulled away and she lost interest, sitting down and picking up a newspaper. 'Like all the English you've no idea what it means to live with your heart. Sometimes I think it's an advantage but not always. How I used to envy those hard, calculating English eyes in London. No, I don't think you're hard and calculating but I do wish you'd be a bit less responsible sometimes—like everyone else around here. It's not rational to be responsible in a place like this.'

It seemed infinitely regrettable that this should have happened only two days earlier, as though things would never be the same again, as though the atmosphere had been poisoned by Jo's death.

Shiuli unclasped her hands from around the coffee cup and with an obvious effort of will brought herself into the present. 'I'm going to phone Rahman to see if we can pick up Jo's things.'

As she walked into the house I noticed she wasn't wearing her bangles. It was the first time I'd seen her without them. They were such an integral part of her personality that I felt I hardly knew her without them. She was upset when she returned from making the phone call.

'What happened?'

'It wasn't Major Rahman—he was unavailable, as they say—but a Major Kalam. He told me that the police at Rangamati would have Jo's things, as road accidents are their responsibility. He said that it was nothing to do with him and that I should go to Rangamati. He was a bit rude really. The bastard.' She was nearly in tears.

'I'll go alone if you like, you can stay here.'

'I'd prefer to go than sit around here with nothing to do except get more miserable.' The corners of her mouth turned up in what was almost a smile.

'We could try phoning first.'

'There's no point. It's practically impossible to get through to Rangamati. It would take us longer than it does to drive there. I'm sure Nazmah will lend us her car.'

In less than an hour it was arranged and Nazmah's driver was waiting for us in the twenty-year-old black Mercedes. I phoned the office of Tarmad in Chittagong, realising that they probably still didn't know of Jo's death. I was put through to the Australian manager and once the difficult bit was over told him where the accident had happened.

'How strange. What was he doing there?'

'That's what the army asked me.'

'Well it is odd. No one's supposed to go into that area without army protection, and not at all at night.'

I asked about Tarith, but he hadn't been seen since he'd left with Jo the week before. The manager suggested that we check with Tarith's relations in Rangamati and gave me their address, adding that he would make enquiries of his own.

Soon we were weaving through the traffic in Feringee Bazar and New Market, Nazmah's driver never faltering in his judgment despite the unpredictable rickshaws. At the top of Jubilee Road, near the Circuit House, we passed a rickshaw with billboards strapped to its sides and a loudspeaker on its roof. The hand-painted pictures showed a sparsely-clad woman.

'Simi Garewal as the courtesan. With Shashi Kapoor. *Siddhartha* at the Ujala Cinema. All this week. Simi Garewal and Shashi Kapoor—' The loudspeaker faded from our hearing as we turned onto the Asian Highway, crossed the railway line and sped through the local bazaars, past the Cantonment and the imposing metalled road to the University—'so the tanks can roll in quickly if there's trouble', Nazmah had told me soon after my arrival. The market town of Hathazari came and went. The road climbed into the low, rounded hills. Paddy fields, betel and coconut plantations gave way to thick scrub and a few dusty teak trees. We passed a group of tribal women trudging uphill and Shiuli told the driver to stop. He pulled the car into the side and we waited for the women to catch up.

They took no notice of us or the car until Shiuli opened her door and offered them a lift. They accepted gratefully, without surprise. There were three of them, two barely more than girls with brightly-coloured clothes and grave faces, who smoothed their skirts carefully as they sat in the back. Their silver necklaces, earrings and intricately embroidered blouses made it seem like an invasion of butterflies into the car.

The older woman's manner was direct but she gave short answers to our questions. 'Yes, we are Chakmas.'

'Are these your daughters?'

'One is mine, the other is my husband's sister.'

'Where are you going?'

The woman gestured vaguely into the jungle and seemed uninclined to explain further, as though the question was impertinent. The girls were silent but occasionally fingered the car's half-open windows or glanced shyly in my direction. On our right the hills dropped away rapidly and in places great ravines had been scoured out by rain-water, exposing the sandy red earth.

'Do you remember when all this was jungle?' Shiuli asked.

'Of course, although I only once came this far west as a girl. We lived in Bhandukbanda and there was no need to go further afield.'

'But now it's under the lake.'

'Yes.'

After only a few miles the woman said that they would like to get out.

'You don't want to go to Rangamati?'

'It's better here.' The statement seemed ambiguous but we didn't press them.

'*Namushkar,*' they all said, pressing their palms together prettily, like Chinese puppets.

'Silly to expect them to be more forthcoming, I suppose,' I said as we continued up the road, patched with light where the sun had found openings in the thick foliage overhead.

'Perhaps they would have been if you'd been alone but for all they know I could be the wife of an army officer, especially in a big car like this.'

Round the next bend the way was barred by a red and white striped pole. We stopped and a soldier told us to follow him to the guardhouse a little way off the road. Others stayed by the barrier. In answer to Shiuli's questions he said, 'Formalities,' and nothing else. In the concrete hut we had to fill in our names, address, nationalities and 'Purpose of visit to Rangamati'. As Shiuli bent to sign the register her sari slipped slightly off one shoulder, leaving it exposed. The dark skin of her arm was accentuated by the whitewashed wall of the hut. The soldier stared at her naked shoulder.

'The Chakma women probably wanted to avoid this check post,' Shiuli said in English, as the soldier escorted us back to the Mercedes. 'Perhaps we'll meet them further up the road.' But we didn't see them again and we were soon driving through the muddy, shack-lined streets of Rangamati, capital of the Chittagong Hill Tracts. Across the grey water of Kaptai Lake which laps the edge of the town the forbidden jungle of the further shore was just visible.

We drove straight to the police station, a new two-storeyed building standing aloof from the tangle of rusty, corrugated-tin shops and houses. At the bottom of the steps leading into the station lay a cow. It chewed impassively as we stepped over it, unimpressed and immovable. A guard stood at the top of the steps holding an ancient Lee-Enfield rifle negligently by its barrel. He hardly bothered to glance at us as we went in.

Shiuli made straight for a curtained doorway marked in

Bengali and English, 'Md. Azher Khan, Superintendent of Police.' I followed her inside. The superintendent sat behind a glass-topped desk, impressively empty apart from a Singapore Airlines pen set. His belly bulged monstrously and kept him an inconvenient distance from the desk should he have wished to sign a chit or write a report. Around the desk were three other men and in front of each a half-finished cup of tea. They rose when they saw me and offered me their chairs. Shiuli promptly took one and I too eventually sat down. The superintendent didn't look at us but picked his teeth with a matchstick until the bustle had died down. He then raised his heavily jowled head towards me enquiringly, baring several gold teeth in what could have been a smile.

Shiuli talked. 'We've come to collect—'

The superintendent's plump hand came down sharply on a bell and simultaneously he shouted for two cups of tea. He transferred his gaze to Shiuli. 'Yes?' he said, as though he'd been waiting politely for her to begin.

'We've come to collect my father's personal effects. Joseph Katchyan: he died in a car accident near Laxmichari two days ago. He had various pieces of luggage with him.'

The superintendent regarded her with distaste for a moment and then turned back to me. 'Why you coming police station? This army matter, not police. It is nothing for me.'

'But Major Kalam at the Chittagong Cantonment informed us that it was your affair,' Shiuli told him, 'and not the army's.'

The superintendent ignored the interruption although his eyes, already set deep in the fleshy face, seemed to retreat further at the mention of Major Kalam. 'There's nothing I can say for army. I am knowing nothing about this Kachin person or his most unfortunately auto accident. I am most sorry to be informing you.'

A peon in a grubby white uniform and bare feet entered nervously with two cups of tea. After a moment's hesitation he put one down in front of me and the other in front of the superintendent.

'Not for me, you half-witted son of a pig, for the lady.'

The superintendent bared his teeth again as he stood up to pass the cup across the expanse of desk, sweating profusely at the effort. He remained standing as we drank our tea.

'But you must know something about it,' I protested, 'the army told us you'd know.'

'Charming sir,' began one of the other men. 'In this matter the superintendent is hapless. If you are requiring other assistances then please come, but he is in a fix for although he is police he is knowing nothing about most unfortunate accident.' He gestured elegantly at the gross form of the superintendent standing like some overripe jack-fruit, ready to disgorge its evil-smelling, entrail-like seeds onto the jungle floor.

'What about accident records?'

The superintendent sat down again with a sigh and began to talk very rapidly and loudly in Bengali. 'Yes, there are accident records but Laxmichari is a long way from here and they won't arrive for at least a month. Then the record must be verified and witnesses must be brought forward.'

'There won't be any witnesses—'

'There are many formalities anyway.'

A man with mirrored dark glasses and a moustache nodded sagely and spoke to me confidentially in English. 'You see he cannot be helping you because he has no knowledge of the matter you are speaking about. That is what he is saying. No knowledge because the accident record is not arriving. That is he cannot be helping you kind sir, or your kind madam. It is jam.' He brushed imaginary dust off his turquoise shirt.

'I am suggesting that you go to the army's Brigade Office. It is only five minutes by motorcar from here,' chimed in the first one again. 'They will most possible be able to be helping you.'

The three men ushered us out and offered conflicting advice as to the quickest route to the Brigade Office. The man with dark glasses watched until we were over the cow, and waved.

'He didn't know anything did he?' Shiuli asked as we clambered back into the uncomfortably hot Mercedes. 'If he had he'd have been more careful about allowing us to disturb the army. I don't suppose he knows much about anything that goes on around here unless it's going to make him money.'

11

WE DECIDED TO find a room and to shower before going to the Brigade Office, and Nazmah's driver took us to the Paradise Hotel. Set on a hill slightly above Rangamati, the hotel's rooms overlook the lake and bougainvillaea sprawls up over the porch. The garden contains a dry pond with an ugly concrete sculpture in the middle, and rusty, municipal-type railings obscure the flowers from view.

The reception counter inside was dusty and we rang the bell several times before an old man in a torn khaki shirt and a green *lungi* tied up between his legs shuffled in from the back. There was so little flesh on his face that the stretched skin exaggerated each bump and hollow. Two or three days' growth of white stubble added to his grey and haggard appearance.

'There's no one here. It's the off season. The boss has gone to the mosque.' He spat a mixture of saliva and red betel juice into a pot holding a dead fern. 'He probably won't be back for a couple of hours. What do you want?'

I could barely understand his dialect but replied in Bengali. 'We want a room.'

'What's he say?' the man asked Shiuli.

'He says we want a room.'

'I'm only the gardener,' he grumbled, 'I can't take responsibility for giving you a room.'

'We'll take full responsibility. Which is the coolest?'

'I don't know. I don't sleep in them, do I? For the foreigner?' He jerked his head in my direction. 'One room?'

'For us both. One room.'

He spat again. 'There's a room on this side which never gets the sun, it's probably the coolest but I don't know the number.' He looked vaguely at the keys behind the counter and licked his lips nervously.

'It's all right, we'll say we took the key ourselves,' Shiuli reassured him.

He brightened up. 'It may be room eleven.' He took the key and then looked doubtfully at Shiuli as though to ensure that he could trust her should anything go wrong.

'I'll take the key.' She put her hand out. The colour of their skins nearly matched.

'I could make you some tea,' he suggested kindly, leading the way down a dimly lit corridor and up some stairs. His legs were thin, the muscles twisted into knots and lumps. Dust and empty cigarette packets lay everywhere. 'Filthy mess, but of course they're all permanent employees, don't have to work if they don't want to. I've been here longer than any of them but I'm still only temporary.' He spat over the open balcony. 'Could you help me? Perhaps you have some relation in the government?' There wasn't much hope in his voice.

'No relations like that I'm afraid but I can try to do something,' Shiuli replied.

'I've still got six children at home. Four daughters. What a life. My name's Mohammed Jalil, gardener first grade.' His shoulders straightened a little. 'You won't forget will you? Mohammed Jalil.' It was the pleading of one who's been kicked all his life, like a dog which only knows how to cringe.

Shiuli unlocked the door to room eleven and we went in, Jalil stayed on the balcony. The room was warm and musty but not stifling. I switched on the fan but turned it off again when hot air which had gathered near the ceiling began to circulate. The bathroom was dingy and dirty, cockroaches scuttled away when I forced open the door, swollen in its frame by the humidity. I turned on the shower and it dribbled unpleasantly warm water, but a tap below it worked and a bucket of cool water stood ready for use.

I went to collect our things from the car and tipped Jalil who followed me down. The driver was waiting with the bags at reception and Jalil bent to comply with his brusque order to take them upstairs but I said I'd do it and told the driver to find himself somewhere to stay, and to return in two hours.

The sheet on the bed was stained and moths or cockroaches

had eaten two or three holes in it. We ate the *shingaras, jalebis* and bananas which Shomela had packed for us. Jalil soon reappeared with two cups of sweet, milky tea on a tray.

I watched Shiuli take the length of sari off her shoulder and straighten the creases before untucking the folds which hung at her waist. She unwrapped herself, passing the cloth around her body, each circle increasing the yards of material in her hands. This process of removing a sari fascinated me. It was done with such slow deliberation and concentration, like a studied, formal dance, the moves practised and refined over centuries. The last fold came loose, and draping the heavy length of silk over the edge of a chair, she put her hands behind her back to unhook the sleeveless blouse, throwing back her head at the same time to get her hair out of the way.

'Why aren't you wearing your bangles?'

'They were annoying me last night so I took them off and forgot to put them back on this morning.'

It was a half-truth at best but I said nothing.

Her blouse too came off, the insubstantial grey-green silk seeming to float in her hands. She wore nothing beneath it. She stretched the elastic of her long white petticoat, pulled it over her head and then stepped out of her panties. The triangle of glossy hair, a deeper shade of black than her skin, reflected little pinpricks of light. Taking a towel from her bag she went into the bathroom and gasped as she splashed herself with water from the bucket.

After I too had washed off the dust and sweat of our journey, we lay on the bed. Only our fingertips touched, it was too hot to be closer.

'We haven't seen a single tribal since we arrived in Rangamati,' Shiuli said, 'apart from the ones we picked up on the way here. Jo brought me here once as a child and I remember that they were everywhere then. This was their town and there were more tribals than Bengalis. Rangamati wasn't much more than a large bazar; the dam was still being built and the land in the valley was full of paddy fields, villages and a Buddhist temple which we went to look at. It was a pagoda built out of wood and very dark inside. As my eyes got used to the gloom they noticed little gleams of gold, like revealed secrets. The gleams resolved themselves into a line of Buddhas, sitting cross-legged, one palm upraised and the fingers of the other hand touching the earth. The biggest of them all, in the middle, was fine-featured and well-proportioned. In front of him were numerous offerings of flowers on brass trays and dozens of incense sticks, some still burning. The mingled scents of flowers and incense, the silence and the darkness, gave the place a peculiar atmosphere, both sad and compelling, like a ballad.'

She paused to light a cigarette.

'The hills here seemed enormous to me. I imagined the Himalayas to be a bit similar. Jo used to tell me stories of his school days in Darjeeling. Stories about the long journey by paddle steamer from Chittagong to Calcutta, then north by train to Siliguri in the foothills of the Himalayas, from where a miniature railway with a ratchet mechanism crawled up to Darjeeling station at eight thousand feet. The school *tongas* would be waiting to take them the last few miles and they used to bribe the drivers to race, although it was forbidden because the road was so narrow and dangerous. It wasn't until I flew the length of the Himalayas on my way to London that I understand what he was talking about, or why it took so long to reach Darjeeling.

'We came to the Hill Tracts once again, just before I went to London. At that time Jo worked for Lewins, the tea people. The dam was finished and the lake had filled up. The company owned a houseboat at Kaptai which we stayed on. It was a sad time because I was going to England and didn't know what to expect; Jo couldn't help me because he'd never been further than Delhi. On the first morning I woke up to find that he'd filled the main cabin with scarlet krishnachura flowers and dozens of jasmine garlands. In the evenings we'd sit on the roof, talking and watching the black and white kingfishers hovering above the lake. They'd suddenly close their wings tight around themselves and drop vertically into the water, appearing a few moments later with a flash of silver in their sharp beaks. He was at his most open then and told me things about himself which I'd never heard before.

'We stayed a week. One day we crossed the lake to Jokha Bazar in a dug-out. It was a pretty place and exciting to see the tribal women, with flowers in their hair, buying and selling cloth, fruit and spices. I wanted to buy some silver bangles from an old woman. Her face was so wrinkled it looked as though it might suddenly crack and fall apart like a broken windscreen. I began to bargain for them but Jo came up and stopped me. I was furious and we stood arguing in the middle of the bazar. I nearly bought them anyway, but when he gave up trying to dissuade me and turned away I caught something in his eyes, a hurt which I'd never seen there before. I felt ashamed and realised that he had some reason even if I didn't know what it was. I went to him and took his arm and we walked back to the dug-out.

'That evening on the roof of the houseboat he produced a box from his pocket. I thought it would contain the bangles I'd wanted to buy, that he'd sent someone back for them. I was wrong. The box did contain bangles, but the ones I unwrapped were different and finer than any I'd seen before. I put them on and he kissed me roughly. There were tears in his eyes.'

'What are they?' I asked, running my hands over the sleek skin of her shoulder. She turned away from me onto her side and didn't reply immediately. Thinking she wasn't going to tell me any more my eyes closed and I heard the rest through a haze of sleepiness; she talked as though to herself and in the silent room her voice took on the same measured rhythms as that of a village story-teller.

'When he was thirty, Jo told me, he met a married woman called Mukti. Her husband was a businessman, very wealthy. They'd travelled in Europe and she found Chittagong dull but her husband insisted that they stay. His business kept him occupied for much of the time and Jo used to visit her in a house they owned outside the city. It was a zamindar's palace which had been in her husband's family since the time of the Permanent Settlement. They were Hindus officially but in practice had little to do with religion, although he was peripherally involved in the Brahmo Samaj. It was 1946. Jo was fascinated by her. He'd won himself a dangerous reputation in respectable society and one outraged husband had even tried to kill him but he told me that he knew it would be different with Mukti from the first time they met. He'd asked in his half-mocking way whether she was bored.

' "I try not to be," she said, "because boredom leads you into things you wouldn't do otherwise and which you regret afterwards. But yes, sometimes I'm bored."

'She was serious, there was nothing coquettish about her. Jo found that honesty irresistible, the refusal and the invitation rolled into one. As he got to know her better and to be more and more in love he discovered that it was a characteristic answer and one of the sources of her power. She gave generously of herself but could withdraw into aristocratic reserve in a flash, a smile almost breaking through. Nobody frightened her—Jo once saw her at an official reception turn at some remark made by the Chittagong Collector and fling, "How arrogant you are!" at him across a roomful of people. It wasn't the sort of thing Bengali women were supposed to say to the most important British official in the city.

'Of course people talked about their affair and stopped inviting her to their parties, but she found that a relief. There wasn't much they could do to Jo because he'd never been welcome anyway. Mukti's husband was making money too fast to care about what she did and when he was at home he preferred to sit in the *jolshaghor* with his cronies, drinking and watching the Nautch girls dance.

'Mukti opened Jo's eyes to many things, he said. Until then he'd been a renegade, whoring and gaming with his friends and making life hell for the ICS officers. Mukti gave him another window on life, introduced him to Bengali music and poetry, made him appreciate the culture he'd grown up in but been taught to be contemptuous of.

'It lasted two years. In '48 came Independence and the massacres of Moslems by Hindus and Hindus by Moslems.

Mukti refused to leave either Moslem East Bengal or the great house with its high ceilings and marble floors. It was typical of her; firstly, she didn't want to be separated from Jo and secondly the possibilities of Independence excited her. One day a communal battle broke out in the village near the house. Who started it no one could say, or rather all said it was the other side. Mukti drove there through the flames and smoke from burning houses and haystacks. Men with knives and guns were running everywhere and she could do nothing to stop it, but she took a group of terrified women and children into her car then drove back towards the house. Nobody quite knows what happened next, but their unrecognisable bodies were found in her burnt-out car the same evening.

'The bangles Jo gave me had belonged to Mukti. She'd left them in Jo's bedroom by mistake the day before she was murdered. He put them away and never looked at them again, he said, until I unwrapped them in front of him.

'That evening we drove home to Chittagong and I left for London within the week.'

Shiuli was quiet, then pressed her face against mine. Her body was convulsed with sobs and her tears wet my cheeks. We lay like that for a long time, my arms tight around her, as though I could take some of her grief into myself.

'I took the bangles off last night,' she continued when she was more in control, 'as a symbol of mourning but also, I can't explain this, because they burnt me. It was as though they were being heated from inside. It lasted only a second or two but I pulled them off immediately. Hysteria perhaps but they left burn marks. Look.'

On either side of her wrist were smooth indentations, each a little more than a centimetre across.

'Were you dreaming?'

'No, I was wide awake, lying on my bed, trying to empty my mind when they suddenly ... got hot. There's no other way I can describe it. They were telling me to take them off—' She started at a loud knock on the door and whispered, 'Get rid of them. Send them away.'

I pulled on a *lungi* and half-opened the door. It was Jalil.

'Your driver's here.' He tried to peer into the room. 'Driver,' he repeated, holding an imaginary steering wheel in front of him in case I hadn't understood. I thanked him and locked the door again.

I lay down again and folded Shiuli in my arms. There had been few occasions when I'd felt myself stronger than her.

'You go, I can't face it,' she said.

Outside the heat and humidity took my breath away and I burnt my fingers on the car door. The light cotton shirt was already stuck to my back. Suddenly it seemed ridiculous to be in Rangamati chasing around for a few worthless bits and pieces which had once belonged to an Armenian called Jo. A watch, a couple of rings and a suitcase full of old clothes, little else. Why had we come? To get away from the house and its memories perhaps, but for Shiuli there were as many memories here in Rangamati. I pondered over the business of the bangles. There had been marks, possibly even burn marks but ... I gave up thinking about it and swore to myself at the senselessness of it all, of Jo's death, of this trip to the Brigade Office, and at the heat. I was glued to the worn leather seat and felt as though I'd trapped myself into another round of formalised conflict with a moribund bureaucracy.

It was time to leave altogether. An era had come to an end with Jo's death. I pictured a flat in London with a view of plane trees which had just burst coolly into leaf. A park opposite where crocuses and daffodils grew. In the summer, at weekends, we'd have a stall at Camden Lock, selling jewellery and cloth from Bangladesh. In winter we'd take a bus through the snow to the bookshops in Charing Cross Road and Great Russell Street. Or we'd just walk around, hand in hand, and no one would notice or care. Sometimes we'd go to the zoo or play with the machines in the Science Museum like children again. Shiuli would become a successful barrister, a QC even, but absurdly that wouldn't matter to us. We'd stay in the same small flat with its view of trees and we'd be happy, nothing would be able to touch our happiness.

The car stopped at a pair of imposing metal gates, painted white, and once again I had to get out and fill in my name, nationality and nature of business. I was searched carefully and thoroughly, then the car and finally we were waved through.

* * *

When I returned from the Brigade Office a plump man sitting sleepily in the hotel lobby waved towards the hotel register and asked me to fill it in.

'Later,' I said angrily and marched past him. I'd had enough of forms and registers for one day.

The air hung thick and still like a damp cloth and I could feel the first slight itchings of a prickly heat rash across my chest. I tried to relieve the itching by splashing myself with water from the bucket in our bathroom as I told Shiuli what had happened. The water only exacerbated the problem.

'I told the soldier at the gate that I wanted to see Major Rahman, which seemed to open a few doors, but he wasn't there so I was shuffled back and forth while they decided what to do with me. I finally got to see a Colonel Chowdhury. He was young to be a colonel.'

'There's a high mutual assassination rate among officers.'

'I suppose so. Anyway he was friendly but not very helpful. I told him about Jo and Major Rahman and the police. He seemed uncomfortable, as though he knew the story already and it embarrassed him. When I finished he said he believed that Major Rahman had what we wanted but that he himself had no power in the matter. I questioned that and said that as a colonel he must have more power than a major. He became a little defensive and blustered about different commands but ended up by saying, strangely, "In some ways Major Rahman has more power than me." He fiddled with some papers on his desk, then stood up and said that he was busy, that he had no more time left. So I came back. There didn't seem to be anything else to do.'

'I'm sick of the whole thing. If only we didn't have to go and see Tarith's relations.'

'We might as well find them if we can. I don't much like the idea of a two-hour car journey tonight. It's a worse alternative than staying. We can leave early in the morning, when it's cooler.'

'Yes. I'm sorry, I feel confused, a bit lost without Jo. I mean he's always been there, always always. I can't get used to the idea of not seeing him again. All last night I tried to imagine life without him, but I couldn't do it.'

I lay down beside her, exhausted by the heat and the day's events.

'I couldn't do it because he's been my life. In a way I've done everything for him, for his approval or at least acknowledgement. Even you were somehow someone Jo felt I should have. I mean as a lover. He didn't want me to get married but I know he thought I should have a lover. I got closer to you than I meant to, though. Now that he's dead I don't have to bother about anyone else in the same way.'

'And me?' I asked, stung by the implication of what she'd said.

'Oh Charles I don't mean I don't care about you, I just said that I did, but Jo was a part of me. I grew up into his ideas, thoughts, stories and life. I couldn't not bother about him even if I wanted to. With you I retain myself, it's important that I do so.'

I slept fitfully and half-remembered, half-dreamt of going to renew my visa. There were no copies of the requisite form in the dusty office, piled high with files done up in blood-red tape, and I had to type it out myself. No one was prepared to help me and the jungle crept in through the windows and doors, snakes slithered over the papers and typewriters, leaf mould rotted underfoot. When I woke it was dark. Cicadas scratched the surface of the night with their constant hum.

I looked out of the window and saw lightning flash in the distance, in the depths of a cloud, charging its bulk with a weight of light and shadow, and then spitting suddenly earthwards with the swift, deft accuracy of a striking snake. I waited for the rumble of thunder, absently counting the seconds but it was too far away, over in Burma or beyond the Lushai Hills and towards the Blue Mountain in Mizoram. The jangle of rickshaw bells tore through the cicadas' interminable drone and then the town was quiet again, not even the pariah dogs barked. Everything waited for rain.

Shiuli's bare arms slithered around my chest from behind and she pressed herself up against my back. I turned in her arms. Our bodies were slippery with sweat. She fell back onto the bed, her hands sliding down my arms to my fingers, and pulled me down on top. Her body, the skin sleek and shiny, tasted salty and primitive. Strands of her long hair stuck flatly to one shoulder and got tangled in our mouths.

'*Harammi*,' she muttered in my ear, biting the lobe. 'Despoiler of innocent women, *Giaour*.'

'Shameless houri, odalisque, Mohammedan harpy.' The syllables came with each breath.

'Infidel Christian,' she got in quickly.

We gave up trying to converse, even in insults, and lost ourselves in the sensual slip and slide which somehow took over, disallowing the intrusion of all else, even the disquiet which sifted and silted in the slow currents of thought.

12

'I'M NOT A Moslem,' Shiuli said as we went downstairs.

'And I'm not an infidel or a Christian.'

She laughed for the first time in two days.

The manager stood behind the reception counter looking stern, the guest book in front of him. Shiuli walked briskly up to him and started to complain about the dust and dirty sheets. He was taken aback to be attacked in this way by a woman and when she finished he asked feebly who she was.

'That's got nothing to do with it. You ask because you want to know whether I have connections. You're a government employee and have a job to do. You're not doing it properly so I'm complaining. You wouldn't sleep in those sheets, but you expect guests to.'

A sickly, apologetic grin spread across his face.

'If you want to keep this cushy job you should do it better. I may not be able to get you fired but I can certainly get you transferred.'

The poor man started to polish the counter with his handkerchief and to blame lazy servants, but Shiuli interrupted saying that we'd be back for dinner in a couple of hours. His plump face twitched and he protested that the cook was away.

'That's nothing to do with us, we're guests and it's your job to provide us with a meal.'

As we walked down the hill I accused Shiuli of imperiousness in her dealings with officials and servants.

'I just insist that people do what they're paid to do.'

'There are ways and means of insisting.'

'Listen, if you're a woman they don't hear you, and if you're apologetic they think you're weak. There's no option but to force your personality on them. It's about time you knew that.'

A group of rickshaws was gathered around a cigarette stall, its kerosene lamp attracting them like fireflies to water. The drivers lounged in their machines smoking *bidis* and talking softly. One of them, with a red *gumshaw* wound stylishly round his head, saw us, leapt to his feet and raced over before the others knew what was happening. He grinned at us wildly and it crossed my mind that he was slightly mad, or at least mentally unbalanced by years of malnutrition and disease.

'See sights,' he said in English. 'Chakma women keep shop, very good. Buddha temple very good. See sights. Me take see all.'

I replied in Bengali and his face fell. 'We want to go to K. C. Dey Road.'

'Yes, yes, K. C. Dey Road.' He fussed around us and tried to put up the hood to shield us from unwelcome stares or catcalls, but Shiuli pushed it down again and made him laugh by asking whether he thought her so ugly that she should be hidden from view.

'Are you a foreigner too?' he asked with awe as we rolled downhill.

'No. I'm just not scared of *mullahs*.'

'You're a film star perhaps. Have you no father or mother?'

There was a pause before she answered. 'No.'

'No father or mother. *Hai hai!* How terrible. No brothers or sisters either?'

Her voice was tense. 'None. No relations at all.'

He glanced back at me as though he understood why she was with me and felt sorry for her. Then we were into the town; he bent low over the handlebars and raced us through the bicycles, rickshaws, pedestrians and porters carrying prodigious loads on their heads, swerving past them and ringing his bell furiously. We grasped the sides of the narrow seat as he swung us round a policeman vainly trying to direct the traffic, and into a quieter, residential street. Trees grew between tall houses made of wood and corrugated iron. The narrow brick road was unlit by street lamps or shops, it zigzagged past houses and halfway round an oily pond which absorbed rather than reflected the stars. He pedalled on to the end of the road and then stopped, breathing hard.

'You don't want K. C. Dey Road?'

'Yes we do.'

'We've reached the end of it.' He gestured back the way we'd come.

I struggled to read the address in the half-light. 'Number 64 by 1.'

As he turned the rickshaw, another came hurtling up K. C. Dey Road and nearly crashed into us. Swerving past us a pair of mirrored glasses under the hood flashed briefly.

'Blind bumpkin! You'd do better to screw your mother like you do every night than to try and drive a rickshaw,' our driver shouted.

We went slowly back over the bumps and ruts and eventually found the house behind a high woven fence over which jasmine grew in profusion, its white flowers and strong scent attracting bees despite the darkness. We could hear them buzzing, seemingly drunk on nectar, as they tried to force an entry into the narrow-stemmed flowers.

The rickshaw driver shouted and rang his bell. A yellow light moved behind the fence and a woman's voice asked what we wanted.

'I'm the daughter of Jo Katchyan. Your nephew Tarith Lal works for him as a driver. Is Tarith with you?' She added, 'I mean worked,' under her breath and squeezed my hand hard.

There was no reply but a section of the fence was pulled back and a hurricane lamp held up to our faces. We said, '*Namushkar*,' in response to the woman's welcome, asked the rickshaw driver to wait and followed her into a small courtyard of beaten earth, swept as clean as the inside of a house. She was small, only five foot or so, with correspondingly small feet and hands but sturdily built despite that. Her broad face was the same honey-gold colour as Tarith's and she wore a bright pink blouse which partly obscured a thick necklace made of coral and silver coins.

On the wooden steps leading onto a narrow veranda sat an old man smoking a cheroot. He watched us incuriously and didn't reply to our greeting, but hitched up his embroidered *lungi* and coughed. The woman fetched two chairs for us then sat next to the man and lit a cheroot herself.

'What do you want to know about Tarith?' she asked in Bengali.

Shiuli told the story from beginning to end and they listened without interrupting, occasionally puffing on their cheroots.

'We've come because we want to know whether Tarith was with Jo the night before last ... the night Jo died, and if he was then we'd like to check that he's unhurt.' She stopped abruptly like a clockwork toy which has run down.

The woman said something in their language and the man answered sharply, but she gave a long reply and looked at Shiuli once or twice. The discussion went on for about ten minutes before the woman spoke to us. 'We don't know where Tarith is. We expected him back three days ago. We are afraid for him. My husband does not want me to say this but I think it can do no harm. We are afraid that he's been taken by the army.'

Her husband interrupted her, still speaking in their language, and they argued again before she continued. 'Many of our people are taken for no reason by the army. Sometimes we do not see them again. I cannot say any more, we are afraid and we cannot ask the army—they would take us too.' She rose and entered the house, her bare feet slapping firmly onto the wooden boards, returning a few minutes later with four glasses filled to the brim.

Naiz, the Mru woman I'd met eighteen months earlier, had said something similar.

I sipped cautiously at the strong alcohol but it still made my eyes water as it burnt its way down my throat.

'The army said nothing about Tarith. But surely they have no reason to take him?'

'We don't know. Often they don't need a reason.'

'But you must know more than that!' Shiuli protested.

The man spoke for the first time in Bengali. 'We don't know you. You come here and ask questions about the army. You bring a foreigner with you. Who is he? We've heard that a British colonel advises the army, helps them to kill us, the Marma, the Chakma, the Mru, all of us. Kill us in our beds. Perhaps this is him. You come and ask questions about this

Tarith Lal. We do not know him, we know nothing.' He looked away from us and blew out a long stream of smoke.

I pulled Shiuli to her feet. 'We'll go.'

The woman opened the gate for us. 'I'm sorry about my husband, he is bitter about many things. If you hear anything will you tell us?' She seemed about to say more but noticed the rickshaw driver standing in the shadows and withdrew without another word.

We rattled along in silence. At the end of K. C. Dey Road was a parked rickshaw. Its driver watched us with interest and I glanced back as we went round the policeman again. The glow of a cigarette was reflected in a pair of dark glasses beneath the hood. I said nothing to Shiuli, telling myself that paranoia is catching and only a form of self-dramatisation. Our rickshaw driver had also lost his appetite for conversation and was almost surly when we paid him off outside the hotel. As he pedalled away he looked back over his naked shoulder. 'Tribal people are rubbish, you shouldn't talk to them. Not Bengalis and not Moslems.'

'Silly fool,' commented Shiuli.

The manager was lying in wait for us with the guest book open in front of him but we went straight into the dining room. A fan turned above the single table which had been laid, ruffling the clean, white table cloth.

The manager served us himself. His plump body, stuffed into a sky-blue safari suit, was unused to exertion and after filling the table with different dishes he collapsed into a nearby chair, breathing hard and wiping his forehead.

The food was excellent, but I couldn't enjoy it; events, people and conversations spun in my head and, like a broken kaleidoscope which refuses to create a regular pattern, I could make no sense of the pieces. What had Jo's accident to do with Tarith being arrested? If he had been. And why were we being followed? If we were. It all seemed to be getting more complicated rather than less so, and I couldn't help feeling that we were out of our depth.

'This is good,' Shiuli told the manager, which brought him bustling over to our table.

'It's good! Yes? Have more sir. You have eaten nothing.' He looked pained. 'You don't like? This *Illish* fish is very tasteful. My wife very good cook.'

Shiuli groaned.

Why hadn't Rahman given me Jo's things when he had the chance? And why had the body been at the Cantonment in the first place? It didn't make sense for the army to be involved. What reasons had Rahman given? None that I could remember. Why did Major Kamal tell Shiuli that it was a police matter? Perhaps Rahman would be able to explain if we caught up with him again.

When Shiuli finished eating she went into the kitchen to compliment the manager's wife. He sat down opposite me and leant forward across the still uncleared table.

'Where is your motherland?'

I stood up. 'Iceland.'

The manager looked puzzled. 'Switzerland?'

'No, Ireland,' I replied cruelly, in no mood to answer properly. As I left the dining room he shouted after me triumphantly.

'Capital Reykjavik!'

A breeze across the balcony brought the faint smell of jasmine.

Lying on the floor of our room was a piece of paper, folded neatly across the middle. Inside was written, 'If you wish to know more about your father's death come to the animal market near Riazuddin Bazar tomorrow at one o'clock.'

I read carefully through the Bengali again in case I'd made a mistake but there was no doubt about the sense. I turned the paper over, looking for a signature or some sign of authorship, but there were no other marks so I went back to the message. It was written in pencil and although all the letters were the same size some curled up over others, making the words hard to read. It was the hand of someone who wrote fast, an educated person. That was as much as I could deduce.

My initial reaction was alarm, for it confirmed my sense of helplessness, of our being the unknowing protagonists in a plot which would close about us like a trap. I thought about tearing it up and then decided I was being melodramatic. We were neither spies nor part of the 'Great Game'. It was absurd, a joke in poor taste, which didn't deserve to be taken seriously.

Shiuli's response was more simple. 'What else is there to know about Jo's death? But I suppose we don't know much, just that he skidded and went over a cliff.'

'We don't have to go, in fact I don't think we should. It's obviously some kind of elaborate hoax.'

'I'd prefer to go and find out anyway. We don't seem to have got very far today.'

I pulled off my shirt and lay on the bed. The sheets had been changed. 'I feel lost in all this. It's rather like a nasty, mysterious game in which no one gives complete answers.'

Shiuli struck a match and burnt the note on the polished floor, then ground the ashes under her heel. 'This is a nation of conspirators who aren't happy unless they're part of at least one plot and know of two or three others. Don't you know the old joke about three Bengalis on a desert Island?'

'No.'

'Who had formed four political parties?'

I smiled mirthlessly. 'Conspiracy doesn't make me happy, it scares me.'

'But you'll carry on, as you're my lover.'

'Yes, of course I will. I'm only saying that there's something nasty about what we're becoming involved in and I don't like it.'

'Nobody likes death much.'

'God you're stupid sometimes. Jo's dead, a car accident. We want to retrieve his things. Easy. Then suddenly the army, the Shanti Bahini and mysterious notes start crawling out of the woodwork. Don't you see that the story's changed?'

'Yes I do, but the problem is yours. Your English railway-track mind can't take it in because it's not normal, but this country isn't normal, most of the world isn't normal. Only England, and only south-east England at that, is normal. It's not normal to be in the middle of a jungle searching for a dead Armenian's luggage. Nothing's fucking normal.'

Sometimes it seemed that we hardly understood each other at all and I rolled over, my back towards her.

She fell asleep as soon as she got into bed, though she tossed and turned, once giving a great sigh which sounded like 'Jo', stretching out a hand which rested on my hip until she shifted again and it slipped off.

The prickly-heat rash prevented me from sleeping, though I was exhausted. Rain pattered on the leaves outside the window and a cool breeze made the curtains swell like a pair of lungs. I drew them back and watched the shower over the vast lake; the water grey and lifeless in the semi-darkness, concealing the drowned temple which Shiuli had described, the villages, and the rich rice lands, giving nothing in return, not even electricity. Only if the great concrete dam, the turbines and generating station are swept away will there be any justice, I thought. What a devastation that would cause in the plains' villages and the city; millions of tons of water rushing out of the hills. A vengeful ancient god—Oreng—released from the stranglehold imposed by technology.

13

IN THE MORNING we hardly spoke as we packed and were soon in the Mercedes speeding back towards Chittagong. I was tired and tried to sleep but was shaken awake by Shiuli a few miles outside Rangamati.

'Look behind us.'

I looked, but saw only a Landcruiser disappearing up the road.

'What am I looking at?'

'It was Jo's Landcruiser.'

'Don't be crazy. There are hundreds of white Landcruisers around. Why should it be his? Rahman said it was a write-off.'

'It was his. I'm sure. It had no windscreen and there was a soldier driving it.'

'And that makes you think it was Jo's? You're mad. I'm going back to sleep.'

'It was *his* Landcruiser, I tell you.'

'Okay. I'm sorry. I didn't mean you're mad. It's something else to ask Rahman about.'

She wasn't listening to me and had already ordered the driver to give chase. I said nothing more, but stared moodily out of the window into the mist and jungle-engulfed valleys.

We got as far as the army check post before Shiuli realised the futility of pursuit; the Landcruiser had obviously not been stopped. Ignoring the surprised stares of the soldiers who had let us through only fifteen minutes earlier, we turned once again and headed back towards the city.

* * *

We sauntered slowly through Riazuddin Bazar towards the Ujala Cinema. As usual the bazar was seething with people. The path was muddy and piles of refuse rotted quietly in the heat. A destitute woman sorted through the rubbish with her bare hands, picking out scraps of paper to sell and putting any food, however putrid, to one side. Salesman flung down gorgeous brocaded silks, one after the other, for the avaricious fingers of rich women to feel and for their eyes to feast on. Displays of the latest fashion in decorated *burkhas* crowded the entrance to some shops. One in particular caught my eye; it was cerise with white, lacy trimmings and seemed designed to draw attention to the wearer rather than render her invisible and unnoticeable on the street. Men handled bras and women's panties with some embarrassment as they chose these articles for their wives shut away safely at home. The stench of rotten, dried fish, a great delicacy, and shouts of '*Bhai, bhai asun*, come in brother,' greeted me as I peered into the fish market.

Where the main bazar takes a left turn the crowds were at their thickest and in the crush a hand slipped into the pocket where I keep my wallet. I grabbed the fingers, twisting hard at the same time. They were yanked from my grasp and I turned, but could see only indifference on the faces behind me. Faces torn from the scrapbook of the sub-continent: pinched and malnourished, telling of hardship and toil, worry written into the foreheads. Fat, sweaty faces with double chins and an arrogant air. Men with *gumshaws* wound round their heads, women with bright eyes, nose-studs and coloured *tikka* marks in the centre of their foreheads. Dark and light skins; a *mélange* of Bengali, Arab, Arakanese, Dravidian, Persian, Portuguese and Habshi slave blood. A babble of voices, conversing, bargaining and shouting. In the distance I glimpsed a turquoise shirt and mirrored sun glasses before the pressure of the crowd forced me to continue forward into the fruit market.

The shouts of '*Bhai, bhai asun*' increased. Here I was well-known as a prodigious buyer of fruit and one not particularly adept at bargaining. I often came back from the market loaded down with pomelos the size of footballs, fresh lychees from Rajshahi, custard apples or mangos. Shomela invariably found something wrong with the fruit itself or the price I'd paid. Clucking her tongue and shaking her head at my inadequacies she would say, 'Even a child of six could do better than you.'

I stopped at a pyramid of oranges and made a show of inspecting them before muttering that they were too expensive. The man picked a date from a fly-covered mound for me to taste. 'You're very serious today, brother.'

I bought some dates and hurried on, clutching the sticky packet. It was nearly one o'clock.

Riazuddin Bazar debouches onto a piece of rough ground next to the Ujala Cinema. Hand-painted hoardings proclaimed, '*Siddhartha*. Starring Simi Garewal and Shashi Kapoor.'

It is on this piece of open ground that animals and birds from the jungles of the Chittagong Hill Tracts and the mangrove swamps of the Sundarbans are displayed for sale.

A raggedly dressed boy with bare feet attached himself to us as soon as we arrived. His arms and legs were encrusted with dirt and although he must have been at least ten he had the physique of a six-year-old. We tried to get rid of him but he insisted on giving us a tour of the cages and took Shiuli by the hand. 'Only two *taka*, two *taka*. Me friend.'

His presence had the advantage of keeping the other urchins at bay as he had some authority over them, threatening one who tried to take my hand. We agreed to the two *taka* fee, and the others didn't attempt to come close again but watched our friend enviously. Talking in exaggerated terms about the ferocity of the beasts he led us to a piece of rusty sheet metal lying on the ground and lifted a corner. Below it was a pit and in its depths lay the heavy, patterned coils of two or three pythons. A head the size of my hand raised itself at the intrusion of light and a pair of agate eyes stared up at us. The boy dropped the metal with a clang.

The wooden bars of a crate holding a bear were so wide and the animal so cramped that we could see little other than thick fur, a wet, snuffling nose crawling with flies, and curved claws which projected two inches out of the crate; vicious-looking weapons which clacked on the wood like dry twigs in a breeze. We saw langurs, a baboon, a cage full of mongeese moving neurotically around their cramped quarters, and scores of parrots.

'One o'clock. You must follow me,' the boy recited like a lesson well-learnt.

He released Shiuli's hand and ducked around the edge of a broken wall which bordered the site. He ran, urging us to hurry, alongside an open drain overflowing with green scum, behind the cinema and in through a back entrance. The uniformed guard took no notice of us as we went in but I heard the metal gate being pulled shut as we followed the boy up some stairs which were heavy with the ammoniac smell of piss. A fern sprayed out delicately from a crack in the wall. The film's flute music echoed off the cement steps and somewhere an air-conditioner roared, struggling to make headway against the cloying humidity.

The boy ushered us into a small room at the top of the stairs, open to the screen at one end but high above the main auditorium. The air-conditioned cinema was cold in comparison to the temperature outside and the seats were dusty. We seemed to be in some little-used special box, for the owner perhaps or his guests. Simi Garewal filled the screen, her scantily-clad figure holding the audience spellbound and silent.

'I can think, I can fast and I can wait,' the voice of the youthful Siddhartha told her. The courtesan's mocking laughter spilled out like the tinkle of bells on an anklet.

As my eyes adjusted to the half-darkness I made out the glow of a lighted cigar and behind it a figure sitting quietly, watching us. I recognised the shaven head and orange robes.

'Boddhipal?' whispered Shiuli. 'Is it you?'

'It is I, yes. Welcome. *Namushkar*. I cannot stay long and I have many things to say. I'm sorry that your father is dead, it is about the nature of his death that I wish to ask some questions.' He spoke quickly and nervously, fingering the edge of his robe.

'We thought we were going to hear something, not be asked questions, Boddhipal.' I meant it to be light-hearted but it sounded brusque, almost rude.

'It is only by asking questions that we can arrive at the truth,' he answered sharply, as though tired of saying such things. 'Charles, you should not have come. Too many people know you, or know who you are. You would be surprised how many know of the Englishman who teaches at the University. I was in Rangamati yesterday and heard that you also were there—someone recognised you, Charles—that is why I sent the note. It is not wise for me to come to your house now, or for you to come to the monastery. I'm sorry because I have enjoyed our friendship but things are happening which make it impossible for the moment. Perhaps in a few months it will be all right again, I cannot tell. I do not know what occurred at Laxmichari but was told that the night before last villagers were woken by the sound of firing. It lasted a minute at the most and then all was quiet again. No one dared investigate and some, fearing an attack by the army, gathered their possessions together and fled into the jungle for the night.

'You must undertand that I am on the periphery of these events. I hear many things but I am not involved.' He blew a stream of smoke at a mosquito which had settled on his hand and it flew off unsteadily, its body bloated with blood.

'In the morning at least three people near Dabalchari saw a white car like your father's being driven by a soldier. The windscreen was shattered and there were small holes in the driver's door and side-window. I tell you only what I know. The Shanti Bahini is very active near Laxmichari. The army designates it a red zone, which means that they control the roads during the day but nothing else. I don't know what your father was doing there at night. I am also told that his driver was active in the Shanti Bahini. That is all. As you can see I have no answers.'

The film flickered then the screen went blank and the lights came up for the interval. The crowd below erupted in noise. People fought to get outside for a cigarette or to buy *pan* and peanuts. At the same time hawkers came in shouting at the tops of their voices. The painfully distorted nasal voice of a popular singer issued from the loudspeakers.

'I must go now. It is best if you stay until the end of the film and leave with everyone else. No one will disturb you here. It is arranged.'

'But Boddhipal, wait, please. Was Tarith with Jo when—' she stopped. 'With him that night?'

'I am told he was but I don't know what happened to him afterwards,' he replied evenly, picking up his saffron-coloured bag and slinging it over one shoulder.

'Are you saying that Jo was murdered?' The word slipped out by mistake, like the sudden spawning of a monstrously deformed child, and seemed to lie among us silent and watchful.

Boddhipal drew a deep breath. 'I am only saying that the possibility exists. I don't know. We must go carefully in this matter.'

'If you hear anything else?' Shiuli asked desperately.

Boddhipal turned at the door and smiled at her. 'I will be here again in a week, at the same time.' Then he was gone, as silently as a dying spark, leaving only the faint aroma of his cigar and a little smoke which drifted lazily over the balcony and into the auditorium.

Shiuli's face was set in a frown of worry and confusion. 'I knew it was Jo's Landcruiser.'

Boddhipal's information had come as a thunderclap, no less shocking because at the back of my mind I'd known that Rahman's version of events didn't add up. It was too slick, too easy, and I remembered something which had puzzled me fleetingly in the morgue. Jo's face was unmarked, although he'd plunged fifty feet over a ravine. I'd hardly been aware of the thought for a second, it had buzzed through my mind like a blowfly sailing past on a hot afternoon. Murder had never been one of the possibilities I'd examined, and the difference between that and a car accident was too great to take in all at once. It involved a leap of the imagination into an abyss of questions.

My fingers felt sticky, as though with blood; I was still clutching the dates. I offered one to Shiuli but she refused and, without taking one myself, I put the packet under my seat.

The lights went down again and the audience grew quiet in anticipation of a screen kiss between two idols, Simi Garewal and Shashi Kapoor. The print was old and worn and it jerked along, unfolding the story slowly: Siddhartha's climb to riches, his degeneration, his decision to return to the life of a mendicant, and the death of his son.

Shiuli's hand lay lifelessly in mine. She stared out at the screen like a blind person aching to understand from the sound alone. The light playing across her features accentuated the dark shadows under her eyes and the frown of concentration. I wanted to talk, to discuss what Boddhipal had said, but guessed that Shiuli was deciding what to do next. Once decided, there would be little hope of changing her mind.

I began to hate the film's simplistic philosophy and the ease with which Siddhartha went through life. Nothing was too difficult, nothing unattainable, and everyone he met took him seriously, listening to his half-baked ideas and self-regard without so much as a snigger. A parable written by an old German mystic, I thought viciously, who'd understood nothing of this slave-bound society, who'd mistaken the recognition of mutability for wisdom and privilege for freedom. Romance is a kind of disease which creeps up on most of us in the sub-continent who are rich enough to do more than survive, foreigners or otherwise. It provides a manageable frame. I was glad when the film finished and we could leave.

Outside I was stopped by two students who wanted to discuss the merits of the film. They stared curiously at Shiuli and invited us to join them for a cup of tea and a sweet.

'It would be our honour and pleasure.'

'Yes indeed. We know the best place for sweets in Chittagong. It is barely two minutes walking from here,' added the other.

I refused as politely as I could and climbed into one of the many rickshaws, crawling round the entrance to the cinema like flies on rotten meat.

'That's it then. There's nothing we can do now. I don't think we should become more involved. Jo was killed by the Shanti Bahini as a warning to those who are working on the road building project. Tarith probably set it up.'

Shiuli looked at me vacantly as though we didn't know each other and she was surprised to find herself in a rickshaw with me. 'Perhaps that's the answer, perhaps not. We'll see.'

'I suppose Rahman didn't tell me what happened in case the consultants get frightened and pull out on the grounds that it's too dangerous to work there. That would be a victory for the Shanti Bahini.'

'Maybe. That's one explanation.'

'Are there others?'

'Of course. You're providing answers to Boddhipal's questions; possibly the wrong ones.'

'It's the only logical explanation.'

'Boddhipal must have thought of it but if he isn't sure then we shouldn't jump to conclusions either.'

'I want to stop thinking about it altogether.'

'That would certainly be easier.'

I tried to keep the annoyance from my voice. 'It's got nothing to do with easiness. It's bad enough that Jo's dead without having to worry about how he came to die as well.'

'If he was murdered then it's something I want to worry about.'

'Perhaps Rahman told me the Landcruiser was a write-off because the army doesn't want a shot-up vehicle around when they're trying to pass it off as an accident.'

'I don't understand why the Shanti Bahini should kill him. They've always kidnapped foreigners in the past.'

The thought had occurred to me also but to say it out loud was like lifting the lid on a pan of boiling oil. Questions spat out in all directions. I prefered to blanket my welling insecurity.

When we got home Shomela told us that Major Rahman had rung four times. 'He sounded angry and shouted at me because I didn't know where you were. I shouted back and he seemed a little surprised. Stupid man, even if he is an army officer.' Shomela had great respect for the army. 'The food's been ready for hours, I'll have to heat it up again.' She shuffled off to the kitchen while Shiuli telephoned Rahman.

I overheard the end of her conversation. 'We have some questions we'd like to ask you too. Until this evening then.'

She sat down next to me at the table.

'Controlled anger, I'd say. We've obviously done something to annoy him. He's coming at seven this evening.'

The wind had got up again and clouds were piling in from the Bay. Shomela closed all the shutters on the west side of the house as two or three overripe mangos lost their grip in the wind and thudded to the ground. Palm fronds clacked and rustled uneasily and the sky grew progressively darker until we had to put on the lights. Then the rain came sheeting down, blown in on the veranda and cracking sharply onto the steps. Shomela's goat bounded up and into the house. We chased it out again and it stood bleating plaintively in the protection of the mango tree, like bait staked out for a tiger.

I was painfully aware of Jo's empty place at the end of the table, and memories of him seemed to be impressed in the walls of the house itself, as though limned into the soft clay of a young mind. Jo had often been away, but it was difficult to accept that he'd never sit there again, talking loudly, drinking and roaring with laughter. A sudden noise made me look up, and I half-expected to see him standing there, shaking water off his clothes and shouting for his 'favourite daughter' but it was only a flurry of rain breaking onto the veranda.

When we'd finished eating Shiuli went into Jo's room to sort out some of his papers, and a few minutes later Nazmah arrived with enormous bunches of flowers and a bag full of fruit. She arranged the flowers in three big vases but they made little difference to either the spacious room or to my sense of worried impotence.

'Without Jo the place seems dead, a museum, as though all these things died with him,' she said.

I looked around at the faded photographs, books, colonial style furniture and the worn Kashmiri carpet, bought many years before from one of the Afghan traders who had once been frequent visitors to Bengal. In the darkness of the afternoon it was true that these possessions had lost their lustre. They seemed either pretentiously grand, or tawdry.

'What does Shiuli intend to do with the house?'

'You've as much idea as I have, Nazmah. Live here I suppose, I can't imagine her living anywhere else. I know what I'd do with it; tear out all these broken, lifeless things and start afresh. I'd fill this room with light and people it with colours, turn the veranda into an aviary alive with song and the flash of orange and green fly-catchers or golden orioles.'

Nazmah stared at me in bewilderment.

'I'd have children everywere, all colours, rid the place of its age and the unhappiness which has stolen over it, clear out every scrap of this solemn teak and mahogany furniture and replace it with insubstantial cane. Throw parties!' I said, encouraged by her laughter. 'Break a hundred glasses a night and light dozens of flickering smoky lamps every new moon. Make it into a scandal in Chittagong. Invite all the most famous *Bauls* to sing and sitarists to play. Spend the days in political intrigue.'

'Not bad as an ideal, though perhaps Shiuli would regard it as a little regressive; a chasing after an imagined golden past when Tagore came to tea and the battles seemed simple.'

I'd run out of ideas and it no longer seemed funny, so I asked about Rahman.

Her long fingers played with a cigarette before she answered. 'I don't know him well, although I used to be friendly with his wife and still see her sometimes. She's in love with someone else and wants to divorce him. Rahman is in Army Intelligence or something, a high flyer.'

I regretted questioning him about the rumoured massacre at Kalampati; Army Intelligence was not to be taken lightly.

'I don't know why he was interested or involved in Jo's funeral arrangements,' she continued. 'It seems odd, he must have better things to do.'

She dragged deeply on her cigarette and I wondered

whether to tell her about our meeting with Boddhipal but she went on before I had the chance. 'He phoned after the funeral last night to say it had been nice seeing me again and we talked a little about you and Shiuli. He seemed to know most things already. I was surprised but I suppose it's part of his job to keep an eye on foreigners like yourself.'

'It can't be very interesting for him. Did you know that he was in the patrol which found Jo's body?'

'I asked about that also but he didn't want to talk about it, beyond saying that it was bloody and unpleasant.'

'No doubt it was,' I said bitterly.

'Perhaps a better way for the old rogue to die than to slowly fall apart on the veranda saying that no one should attempt to preserve him. He'd have hated being old, sitting around all day with nothing to do except fight with Shomela and Shiuli. He'd have been bored and irascible.'

Again I was tempted to tell her the whole story. I was uneasily aware that I would be dragging her into something which could only worry her or work to her disadvantage. There was no one else to lean on, however, and I began, haltingly, to try and explain what Boddhipal had told us, only to be interrupted by the appearance of Shiuli. She went up to Nazmah and held out the little bas-relief from Pandita Vihara, cupped in her two hands carefully, like a piece of living tissue.

'Take it. He'd have liked you to have it—especially knowing how you disapproved of him taking it.'

Nazmah relieved Shiuli of the dancing figure, redolent of the rich culture which brought it into being, now trapped in the Cantonment's defences. 'I don't really disapprove.'

'It was a good imitation then.'

'No, I was just surprised and shocked the first time I saw her. As I remember we had an argument about preservation, not about the fact of Jo possessing her—it was a *fait accompli* after all. Thank you.'

'We saw Boddhipal this afternoon,' Shiuli said, sitting down, 'and he seems to think that Jo was shot—'

'That's not what he said,' I interrupted.

'No, but it was the implication of what he did say.'

Nazmah didn't move or adjust her gaze from the stone for a long time, then her face lifted slowly towards Shiuli. 'Who by?'

'That's the question. It could hardly be a random killing, could it? Rahman's coming here later and I'll ask him.'

'Do be careful. He's no fool, Shiuli.'

'I know.'

Shomela brought tea on a tray then went down the veranda steps; the faded greens of her sari merged with the variegated and shadowy hues of the garden. Nobody spoke. When Shomela returned she put a couple of fresh limes on the cheap tin tray with its faded picture of a Venetian canal and gondolas, then touched Shiuli's shoulder for a moment before turning back towards the kitchen. A few minutes later, after the last liquid notes of the call to prayer had bubbled into silence, we heard her laboriously reading an Arabic prayer from the Koran. She could not understand a word of Arabic but drew immense spiritual strength from the sound of the words themselves and from performance of the necessary rituals. It was something which seemed to take her out of the narrow world of house and garden she inhabited, and she would not listen to Shiuli's impassioned arguments against Islam, though they shared a loathing of mullahs, referring to them as 'those bearded leeches'.

14

I watched the crows while waiting for Major Rahman to arrive. There didn't seem to be anything else to do. In the space of eighteen months I'd grown fond of them, even though they were noisy, woke me every morning at dawn and had stolen my breakfast toast from under my nose on more than one occasion, swooping off with triumphant cackles. I admired the way they teased and chased away the powerful kite which sometimes settled lazily on the roof of the house. They would hop up to the big bird of prey, heads bobbing in apparent deference and caw loudly or jump into the air and flap their wings in its face, unafraid of the sharp beak and talons.

Rahman wouldn't sit down or accept a drink and walked stiffly up and down the veranda. 'Why did you go to Rangamati?'

'Because Major Kalam told mc we'd be able to collect Jo's things from the police there. It's quite simple, and anyway we're allowed to.'

'What's Kalam got to do with it? He doesn't know anything about this.'

'So it seems. I spoke to him yesterday and he told me that car accidents are nothing to do with the army. Actually he said, "It's not our pigeon." The police don't seem to think it's their "pigeon" either.'

'You're allowed to go to Rangamati. But why didn't you sign the hotel register?'

His interrogatory manner angered Shiuli, who was more used to delivering questions than answering them. 'We forgot. We had other things on our minds. Did you have us followed?'

'You signed the register on the road to Rangamati and we checked the hotels. Normal procedure. The manager of the Paradise said you'd refused to sign.'

I hoped they hadn't maltreated the manager to elicit this information.

'What happened to Jo's things, Major? Surely I'm allowed to have them back, or have they been pawned already?'

The insult brought Rahman up short and he stared at her coldly. 'Of course you're allowed to have them back, but you must follow the correct procedure.'

'Of course. We have some questions to ask you, Major. The police told us that it's an army matter and the army that it's a police matter, so which is it?'

'Most things which happen in the Hill Tracts are army matters.'

'Is that why you told Charles that the Landcruiser was a write-off? Because the army wants to keep it?'

Rahman sat down abruptly and his hands dropped onto his knees, where they straightened the creases in his trousers in an absent-minded way. The electricity had failed again and it was difficult to make out the expression on his face by the light of a single hurricane lamp.

'It is a write-off.'

'But Major, I saw it this morning on the road to Rangamati.'

Rahman fell into her trap, forgetting she was trained at least as well as he was in the art of interrogation. He drew a deep breath and paused dramatically; I was reminded of an actor who has momentarily forgotten his lines. 'What I am about to tell you must go no further. Do I have your agreement?'

We nodded.

'Murder is not a pleasant word and I don't use it lightly. I've seen men murdered during the Liberation War and more recently in the Hill Tracts. In order not to upset or worry either you or Tarmad we decided to explain your father's death as an accident. In reality he was murdered by the Shanti Bahini.'

Shiuli had her next question ready and threw it at him in her best court-room style. 'Why should they murder him?'

It obviously wasn't the reaction he'd expected and he replied slowly. 'We conjecture that they tried to kidnap him, he resisted and they shot him. Your father wasn't someone who simply allowed things to happen to him.'

'What about Tarith Lal? Jo's driver?'

There was an even longer pause and he seemed to be weighing up the possible consequences of giving us more information. 'Tarith Lal was there. He was an active member of the Shanti Bahini. We've been watching him for some time.'

'You say was. Is he dead too?'

'I mean is.'

'If you've been watching him, then did you lose him that night? And how could Tarith drive Jo into an area which all the consultants knew was dangerous, at night?'

His uniform's brass buttons winked in the light as he shrugged. 'We're also puzzled about that.'

I repeated Shiuli's question. 'You weren't following Tarith two nights ago?'

'Unfortunately not. We can't keep track of everyone at the same time. I would have returned the rings and watch later. I'll send a driver with them tomorrow.'

His candid, boyish face made me feel a little sorry for him; locked into a world of suspicion and intrigue in which death was as likely to come from a fellow army officer as from a tribal guerrilla. His next sentence was for me. 'The night before last you asked me about Kalampati. I realise that rumours spread fast in Chittagong but I must warn you that it's unwise to talk about such things, to anyone.'

His official tone surprised me considering the answer he'd given at the time: *murder*, he'd said. Now it sounded as though he was threatening me but he laughed uncomfortably when I voiced the thought.

'No. It's advice, not a threat.' His hands fluttered a little, their shadows leaping up the wall behind like black flames.

'Coming from the army that's the same thing,' Shiuli said angrily.

'It doesn't come from the army but unofficially from me. I haven't mentioned the question to anyone else and I won't, but he should be more careful.'

'Or what?'

'What do you expect me to say? The Hill Tracts, as you know, is a sensitive issue, especially where foreigners are concerned. If they raise questions then they must expect to come under suspicion. It's a matter of the internal security of the state.'

'That's a threat—'

'Shiuli,' I interrupted, 'He's trying to warn me to be more careful, that's all, and you're making it difficult for him.'

'I'm sure he can take it. If he can murder tribal women and children then a few words won't hurt him.'

His response was icy. 'I do not murder anyone. I was not at Kalampati and I hate this war as much as you do—'

'I doubt it.'

'Army Intelligence gathers information. That's my job, not killing innocents.'

'Well someone does.'

'They kill us too. They killed your father, he was an innocent.'

'I'm not sure I believe your story.'

'Shiuli!' I protested, trying to prevent her from saying more.

Rahman stood up. 'You should believe it. It's better if you do, for everyone. It would be a mistake for either of you to become more involved in this thing.'

He shouted through the rain and a soldier came running with an umbrella. He ducked under it and went quickly down the steps. A minute later the jeep's engine roared to life and its powerful headlights blazed through the narrow palm trunks and serried rain. I looked away but Shiuli faced the blinding light until the driver had backed the vehicle out of the compound and we were left with the hurricane lamp's yellowish glow. Shiuli put her hands up to her eyes and rubbed them.

'Why did you say you didn't believe his story? You shouldn't confront the army like that.'

'I don't know. I got fed up with his attitude. He's in the army but pretends to be nobler than his colleagues. "It's not my job to kill innocents. I just gather information",' she mimicked. 'I bet he's just as ruthless as the rest of them but he has a conscience about it.'

'I think he's caught up in something he doesn't like but he can't do much about it. He probably tries to mitigate the worst excesses of the *jawans* and other officers.'

'That makes it worse. He knows that it's genocide up there and feels guilty about it, but he's too much of a coward to stand up against it.'

'It was the Shanti Bahini not the army who murdered Jo,' I said, afraid of the reaction I might provoke.

'I know, I know. I hate them too. But it's the army, the government and us Bengalis who created the problem. Who created the Shanti Bahini in effect. I can't think any more. I'm tired and my head's going round. I'm going to bed.'

As her shadow sank back into the dark recesses of the big room I experienced a sharp sense of loss, as though she'd gone for ever. I nearly cried out to her but the shout died in my throat, finishing as a strangled gurgle, oddly at one with the sound of swirling, eddying water round the house, rushing like dreams into the night and out of the grasp of consciousness.

The veranda looked abandoned. Flakes of whitewash lay along the edges of the walls and water dripped from a leak in the roof, leaving a smudge of green algae down one wall. The drips fell twenty feet and broke apart on the black-and-white tiles, spraying a twisted blood-thorn growing in a pot nearby. Even in the feeble light golden droplets flashed among the plant's long spikes and neat, square-cut flowers.

By the time I went to bed the electricity had come back on but power was low and the fans creaked as they turned. Shiuli was asleep in my bed, a sheet drawn up to her waist.

I drew aside the mosquito-net and climbed in beside her.

'Shiuli, let's go to London. I'm tired of it here. I'll be able to get a teaching job and you could go back to your old firm. We could find a flat overlooking a park. We'd be anonymous again, just the two of us alone together in the city.' She didn't respond but I could tell from her breathing that she was awake and listening. 'We'd have no need of anyone else. Imagine it, Shiuli; nothing to hurt us, nothing to agonise over, no beggars crowding the pavements of our minds, or lepers or half-starved children with accusing eyes. We'd walk in the parks and sing in the rain, that soft London drizzle, and eat crumpets in front of an open fire in winter. The flat would be crowded with books and we'd read to each other—'

'The myth of return,' she said sleepily. 'All exiles have it, even third and fourth generation Anglo-Indians talk of going "home"—to England.' She looked up, brushing aside a strand of hair, and rested her chin on her hands. 'I'm sorry Charles, I can't go back, not now. The last few days have convinced me that this is where I belong. I'm just another immigrant in London, spat at in the streets and abused on buses. The dream would become a nightmare.'

'But there's nothing to hold you here. It's so cruel in this place and you're not free to do as you please. You remember those men at Chand Kebab? Our arrest? Nazmah's ex-husband? You always say that people won't leave you alone. You've survived London before and enjoyed it.'

'Yes, but I have a clearer idea of what I want to do now.'

'It could work in London, Shiuli, I'm sure it could. We'd be happy. You could do whatever you want from there.' I was begging.

'It's not the same. There are issues which have to be fought here, not from some smart office in London.'

'But it's bound to be dangerous. You'll end up in jail yourself.'

She turned her face away and pulled the sheet up around her. 'That's a risk I'll have to take.'

'Why you? Why should you risk yourself when no one else does? One day, perhaps soon, the country will erupt and there'll be no room for humanism then. You'll be caught in the cross-fire.'

'No, I'll be on one side or the other. But that isn't the point. I want you to understand, Charles, but if you're unable to then I can't help. I can't abandon my country and people for you. A few months, or even days ago I might have, but not now. This idea has become important to me, even though it's not yet fully formed. I feel that it's going to take me somewhere.'

'To a cell—'

She covered my mouth with her fingers and began to kiss and caress me, but I couldn't make love, my mind was too taken up with fears and imaginings. Their capillaries had taken hold and were pushing into my brain, clogging the synapses, just as in the high Himalayas where the caterpillar of *Papilio Krishna Krishna*, the rare swallow-tailed butterfly with crimson puddles on its black, ragged wings, nourishes and is deranged by the parasitic fungus *Cordyceps Senensis*. The parasite's hyphae bury themselves in the insect's central nervous system, feeding off and desiccating it until there is nothing left but a blackened skin, resembling more a root than the remains of what could have been a butterfly coasting over the spring and summer pastureland.

Part Four

15

I RESUMED MARKING exam scripts, interrupted by the sudden arrival of Major Rahman two days before. They seemed worse than ever and I skimmed blearily through the damp pages, as often as not awarding marks on the basis of neatness, handwriting or spelling, failing no one. It was an occupation, like those given to the mad, to fill in time, the time before Shiuli's next meeting with Boddhipal. No doubt the rest of the Department would play out the usual charade of doubling all the students' marks so that a reasonable percentage passed. The staff didn't demur at this, for honour was satisfied; they'd done their ritual duty by marking to a high standard and they considered it unfortunate that political expediency dictated that students should pass exams. I daydreamed and wondered at the futility of my work. It was like a return to those endlessly dry, uninspiring days in the Sudan. Three years had gone by and I'd arrived with such optimism. I remembered my first monsoon; I'd watched the pregnant clouds roll in from the Bay, and run out into the rain when it arrived, fully clothed, excited by the elemental power of the storm.

As the week wore on I became fearful, scared to go beyond the quiet, familiar compound and its solid wooden doors. I imagined that Major Rahman suspected us of involvement in the activities of the Shanti Bahini, though why I should think such a thing I couldn't have explained, except in the depths of my mind where perhaps I knew or at least guessed at the truth of Jo's death. I imagined that if I left the house I would be watched, followed, even arrested. Panicking, my thoughts ran this way and that looking for an escape. I regretted asking Rahman about Kalampati again and again. My paranoia was so advanced that one night I was kept awake by what sounded to me like the wild yelling of a fanatical mob echoing over the city, and it was hours before I realised that it was merely dogs baying at the moon or howling in hunger and misery.

Until Jo's death I'd existed in an unreal world which had conspired to make me accept a romantic illusion. The old house with its geckos and faded photographs, my work in dusty, half-empty lecture theatres, the Club and the slums—the city's insane contrasts—and my affair with Shiuli, had all been part of this enveloping hallucination.

Now there were too many people, colours and smells, too much activity and noise. Above all there was too much disease and suffering, and I found that I'd lost the ability to move through the anarchic, cruel chaos with any detachment.

Shiuli was my only sure reference point and I clove to her, suffering agonies when she left the house. She was scornful of my concern. 'You forget that this is my city; it can't shock or surprise me any more and there's nothing to be afraid of.'

At night, if she came to my room, we'd make love or talk but the intensity seemed to have evaporated or sunk into the darkness of Jo's grave. The initiative always lay with her, she seemed to have retreated out of my grasp, into an area of her mind which was purely Bengali and into which I would never be able to follow. Allied to this was a new determination and reserve, a new impatience with me which was frightening. I left her to herself as much as I could. I often stayed awake long after she'd gone to sleep, and would look carefully at her handsome, generously carved features, the wide mouth and strong nose, her mane of hair, and stretch of skin, and wonder how I might induce her to leave.

'Will you never understand?' she asked when I raised the subject again. 'There's nothing I'd like better than to live in ease, lead a comfortable life with a flat in Islington. But I can't at the moment because I haven't tried to do anything here. If I try and fail then I'll have to think again, not before.'

Sometime during that long week she had her hair cut so that it barely reached her shoulders. Once I got used to the more Western appearance I liked it but annoyed her by repeating what Shomela, who hated the change, had said: '*Hai hai!* You look like some cheap Bombay starlet.'

The monsoon held itself in check, restraining the impulse

to deluge and drown the low-lying land. Storm clouds lumbered in from the Bay each afternoon but failed to deliver more than a few insignificant drops. The humidity wearied everything, even the crows ceased to cackle and caw at each other. Overcome with lassitude they sat disconsolate in the shade of the mango tree, pecking at each other bad-temperedly. Only the plants thrived, spreading wildly as though, now that Jo was gone, they could smother the house, bury it with impunity. The ferns beneath the veranda roof grew voluminous, their seeking roots frequently pushed chunks of rotten, blackened plaster off the wall, and their jagged leaves embraced in a strangle-hold. Their evident health and energy awed me; it was excessive and beyond human control and it seemed impossible that such prodigality could be sustained.

My prickly heat grew worse, spreading to my shoulders, back and neck; the red inflammations burnt and itched by turns, driving me mad with the desire to scratch. The only effective remedy was to lie spread-eagled under the fan, but the power was off so frequently that I was rarely able to do this.

* * *

The day of the meeting I watched Shiuli jealously as she dressed, as though suspecting her of a liaison, of going to meet another lover. I tried, with no hope of success, to dissuade her from going.

'It's important that I know what happened to Jo. Important to me. I want to know the details, to know that there aren't any loose ends, like Tarith Lal. Not knowing—'

'You do know but you won't accept Rahman's explanation.'

'It's not that I won't accept it but Boddhipal may be able to throw more light on it than Rahman was able or willing to. We don't know what Jo was doing in Laxmichari, for example. I still don't believe that Tarith deliberately led him into a trap.'

Positioning a chair on the veranda so that I had a clear view through the creepers hanging over the arches, through the palm trees and shrubs to the street doors, I sat like a creature possessed, chain-smoking and waiting for her return.

Shomela shuffled out to tell me that lunch was ready. 'I've just heard a cyclone warning on the radio. It's expected this evening. There's been a massacre in the Hill Tracts also. The radio said eighty Bengali settlers were murdered by the Shanti Bahini last night. The poor things, trying to build a new life and the tribals murder them.'

'Where was it?'

'I forget. Some outlandish name. Eighty people; men, women and children.'

'Perhaps they'd been settled on tribal land, or in a tribal village.'

'They don't have any land, it belongs to Bangladesh.'

'Oh Shomela—' I couldn't go on, I'd run out of energy to argue with her, to argue with anyone.

She glanced at the clouds, bruised black and yellow, thickening above us. 'Do you want your lunch or not?'

'No.'

I heard her clearing the table and then closing all the windows and shutters. Leaves gusted past me and scraped along the veranda from one end to the other. A dry desolate sound.

I looked at my watch constantly during Shiuli's absence, hoping that she wouldn't stay until the end of the film and listening for the groan of the doors' rusty hinges which would signal her return. Sweat crawled down my face and chest like flies, tickling the nerve ends and evaporating. I moved only once, in order to change into a *lungi*.

A few large drops of rain scattered on the dusty steps and fell heavily into the mass of greenery, then suddenly water dissolved the far side of the garden. Within minutes it was hurtling off the roof in spouts and the brick path had disappeared beneath a layer of liquid grey mud. I began to feel cold without a shirt but stayed where I was, as though afraid that Shiuli might not make it across the garden if I wasn't there.

She was away for three hours forty-five minutes, an hour more than I estimated was necessary, and I was biting my nails by the time she came through the gates, her sari flapping crazily in the wind. Absurdly I felt embarrassed by my semi-nakedness and slipped into my room to put on a shirt, re-emerging as she came up the veranda steps. Her hair was plastered to her skull, her sari darkened by water and muddy at the edge. She was shivering and for a second I felt indifferent to her, seeing her as just another woman, not even anyone I knew.

We both spoke at once.

'Boddhipal has seen Tarith.'

'Why were you so long? There's been a cyclone warning.'

She sounded excited, even reckless and it unnerved me, but I followed her into her room. It was, like mine, an almost perfect cube. Two sets of double doors led onto the veranda and windows in the other outside wall overlooked the garden. A pale, diseased light shone through the slats in the Venetian shutters, as though cast through choppy water and seaweed. I lay on the bed as she began to strip off her wet sari.

'Boddhipal was waiting as he said he would be. He'd spoken to Tarith. The army killed Jo, not the Shanti Bahini. They opened fire with machine guns. Several others were killed also. Tarith managed to escape into the jungle.'

I tried to make her explain it slowly but she hardly noticed.

'Tarith didn't want to meet Boddhipal but was eventually persuaded to. I don't know where they met.

'Jo and Tarith had taken a case of explosive from the project stores, Jo had signed it out himself. Nobody questioned it. The engineer, one of the foreign consultants, signing out explosive. Normal. They were going to give it to the Shanti Bahini. Tarith arranged it. After Tarith's family village was burnt down Jo started to ask him about the tribals' problems. They talked for six months. This was their first attempt to help the Shanti Bahini together. They drove to Laxmichari from Khagrachari, where they'd been staying in the *dak* bungalow. It was early evening, dusk.'

She sat heavily on the bed, still in her damp petticoat and blouse, took one of my hands in both of hers and examined it quizzically. I'd seen her do the same thing to Jo; look at his hand as though it were some inanimate object from another age, the purpose of which was unclear.

'Go on,' I said, propping myself up on one elbow and withdrawing my hand.

She stood to remove her remaining clothes and, leaving them in a pile on the floor, climbed into bed. We pulled the coverlet up over us—the tremors running up and down her body gradually lessened in intensity and frequency as she spoke.

'It took them only a moment to unload the heavy case and to carry it off the road. It was too big to carry through the jungle like that so it was going to be split up. While Jo turned the Landcruiser Tarith helped the Shanti Bahini men to unpack the case. The next moment a machine gun opened up. Tarith dived into the jungle. It was over in no time. Jo was killed outright and three Shanti Bahini men are missing, probably dead.'

She looked me in the eyes for the first time since starting the story, but the dark irises sheered away quickly, like frightened birds. I put an arm around her cold, damp shoulders and pulled her clumsily towards me.

'Tarith asked Boddhipal to tell me that Jo would always be remembered by the tribal people for his bravery.' She was keeping her voice under control by an effort of will.

I muttered a few words of encouragement, soothing nonsense, but her nervous compulsion to talk was greater than her need for reassurance.

'He told me, in a way, what he was planning to do. When we were alone one evening he whispered something which didn't make much sense at the time, something about swopping companies, I think those were the words he used, and going to work with people he felt more at home with. Typical of him to put it like that; not to define it as a political act but as one of sensibility.'

I wondered whether it wasn't some retributive instinct, a memory of the massacres in Anatolia and the flight from Turkey, which urged Jo to act as he did, to defend a cultured and beleaguered people. But now, when I remember him clearly, I realise it was an unlikely supposition. As Shiuli had said, he thought not in historical terms but in the personal. He must have known that it was at best a gesture and that the end would come quickly, at the point of a rifle or in an army cell.

The implications of Boddhipal's information began to filter past my worry about Shiuli, and fear invaded my mind like a flood which washes into every crevice, tears up solid structures and then abandons the unrecognisable, twisted wreckage. Jo working for the Shanti Bahini. *It would be a mistake for either of you to become more involved in this*, Rahman had warned. He had been testing me, I had no doubt about it. We had been followed in Rangamati and Chittagong, it wasn't my imagination. Innumerable questions formed and dissolved like badly fixed photographic prints.

'What were they going to do with the explosive?'

'Blow up a bridge or two. Perhaps electricity pylons taking power from Kaptai to Chittagong—though you wouldn't have thought they could make the supply worse. There wasn't enough to do much more than that.'

'Why should the army want to keep it secret?'

'What? Shooting a foreigner, even an old Armenian, makes news if he's shot by government troops, especially if he's turned guerrilla after living peaceably for seventy-odd years. The less publicity the better as far as the government's concerned.'

'Do you think Rahman did it?'

'No. It was men from the local army camp, led by a certain Captain Jilani. The tribals know all the local army officers by name—which ones are killers, which ones to fear for other reasons and so on. Jilani's one of the worst apparently. The kind who rapes and kills without a second thought.'

Now surely she would come to London. Boddhipal's information would have made her change her mind. 'We must leave, Rahman's already suspicious of us. It's dangerous to stay here any longer.'

Shiuli ignored the statement. I knew then that I'd lost, that Jo had been too powerful for me, even in death.

'From the cinema I went to see one of my colleagues. We talked about the possibility of taking legal action against the army and government over the Hill Tracts: murder, torture, rape, arbitrary arrest, illegal confiscation of land, religious persecution, everything.'

I said nothing but she must have guessed what I was thinking.

'It's not that dangerous. It depends on how it's done. We have enough connections with lawyers in London and New York and with the international press to make it difficult for them to lock us up.' She spoke slowly and reasonably, watching my face, absorbing my agitation.

I tried to match her calm, even tone. 'But the government, the army, or both will get fed up with you sooner or later, and then you'll be thrown in jail to rot.'

Shiuli smiled.

'What are you smiling at? I'm serious.'

'I know you are but the situation seems to draw dramatic clichés from you.'

'Please give up the idea.'

'I can't.'

'Or won't?'

'If you like. Listen. Jo fought in the only way he knew—with his fists. That's not my way but I can still tackle the problem head on.'

'And be charged with sedition.'

'It's not as stupid as you seem to think.'

'Don't you see that you're blindly following Jo?'

'You're wrong. Jo had his own ideas and put them into practice. This is the kind of legal work I've been looking for, preparing myself for since I came back. Jo may have shown me the way but I'm not being led by him.'

I played my last card, without much hope or conviction. 'I shall leave if you do this work. It's madness.'

She looked at me sadly for a moment then rolled off the bed and from her bag produced an envelope addressed to me. 'It's from Boddhipal.'

The imagery of Buddhist thought with which Boddhipal scattered his letter was too far from the present and the immediate for me to identify with and, after skimming through it, I crumpled the single sheet of airmail paper and threw it into the wastepaper basket in my room.

16

THAT NIGHT I made love to Shiuli with a desperate, unimaginative violence which shocked us both. It was as though I wanted to punish her for provoking the conflict of emotions which so confused me. I had no desire to leave her but equally I didn't want to be thrown in jail, interrogated or tortured. Rahman's manner and questions were making increasingly good sense to me. His statement at the graveside, *It's a hateful war but Dhaka refuses to negotiate,* had been an invitation to express an opinion, and in a way I'd complied by asking about Kalampati. Perhaps my naïveté had convinced him of my innocence, but if Shiuli did as she threatened his suspicions would redouble.

She pushed me away and sat up. 'You hurt me. You're behaving as though I'm a stranger, someone you don't know and don't care about. I think you're doing that horribly English thing, what I call the polite retreat. Pretending that everything's the same but planning how to escape possible disaster; a creeping away in snow shoes.'

'I'm sorry,' I replied, aware of the inadequacy of the response.

The rain and wind had ceased battering the house and we became conscious of a distant hum; human voices raised in anger or excitement. It gradually increased in volume and we opened one of the veranda doors to peer out and listen. Reflected on the upper storeys of houses on the other side of Armenian Street were the flickering lights of torches and the distorted shadows of hands and faces.

We could make out few of the hoarse cries. '*Zindabad! Zindabad!* Victory!' was clear, and this was followed by a chant of which the only discernible words were 'Death!' and 'Burn them!' The shadows and clamour gradually faded away, leaving the night curiously still and silent as though it were waiting for something dramatic to happen, to break through the heavy flannel of humidity and rouse the world.

I found myself talking, trying to explain why I wanted to leave. 'You don't understand the strain of living in a place where people are abandoned like bits of old sacking on the streets, where every day I do something I'm ashamed of: ignoring a beggar, shouting at a rickshawwallah, anything. It's begun to bite harder since Jo's death and I can't live if I'm going to be followed around by Special Branch and Army Intelligence as well.'

'Of course I understand, but it's life. As I tried to say the other night in Rangamati there are few places in the world where, if you're aware and honest, life isn't a constant battle with your conscience and understanding. Perhaps this country is harder than some places but most of the world is more like Bangladesh than Europe. Why do you think Jo started to help the Shanti Bahini? Or why I want to do the same thing in a different way?'

'I don't know. It's madness.'

'Because it's the only rational response. Helping individuals is wasted effort; you have to do something on a bigger scale.'

'Jo wasn't political. He didn't think like that.'

'Perhaps he had to eventually.'

'I think he did it because of you. He wanted to win you back from me in some way.' As I expressed this idea, which had come unbidden and unexpectedly, I was conscious of the desire, still lurking in the shadows, to inflict pain. 'You'd given yourself to me, not completely perhaps but enough to make him feel abandoned.'

I still don't know how true it was.

'I drove him to it, killed him in effect. Is that what you mean?'

I should have been warned by her sudden stillness but I didn't know if that's what I'd meant. Hesitantly I tried to expand on the idea; it had begun to sound reasonable. 'He was trying to win back your respect, or at least do something he thought you'd approve of. You were all Jo had.'

She looked across the room at the statue of Nataraj in his circle of fire: an incarnation of Siva the Destroyer. 'If you want to leave me or to leave Chittagong, then do it but don't torture me in the process.' She spoke each word singly, as though it pained her to talk at all, biting back the tears.

'Shiuli, I have to leave, my emotions are in shreds. It's as though a vulture came and ripped off a bit more every day. I can't be open to any more pain or paranoia and this whole country is in agony. My emotions are hacked from me whether I like it or not. I don't control them any more. They switch back and forth between love and hate like some demented traffic light.'

'You mean you're going to rebuild those English emotional barriers?' Suddenly she was angry. 'Then don't do it near me!'

Her body tensed and I thought she was going to throw herself at me, to attack me with her nails and teeth, but, pulling aside the mosquito-net, she stepped off the bed and a few seconds later I heard the bolts of her bedroom doors being slammed into place.

Why couldn't she understand that while emotions challenged her *I* was crushed by them? That love, our implication in Jo's death, fear of what she was becoming involved in, and the enforced callousness of everyday life, the cruelty and indifference, had worn me down.

I got up to retrieve Boddhipal's letter from the wastepaper basket. An idea had begun to form, like dust settling on a sunlit table. If I was to regain my equanimity and win back control of my emotions I had to find a place where nothing could disturb me.

'Dear friend Charles,' I read,

Shiuli told me that you want to leave Chittagong. In case you go before we are able to meet again I take this opportunity to say goodbye. There are still many things we could talk about, and perhaps we will sometime in the future. I hope that our discussions have been and will be of use in your life. Do not lose sight of the goal: the development of true wisdom. This is not the wisdom of the intellect, which is aware of and stresses its individuality, but the wisdom of insight into the true nature of all things. An insight which carries one towards Enlightenment, a knowledge and understanding of impermanence.

    We rest.—A dream has power to poison sleep;
    We rise.—One wandering thought pollutes the day. . . .

    In this world where all is mutable (do you remember teaching me that word?) remember that what is known as reality, this life is a film of petrol over an ocean. Its pretty colours and changing patterns attract us but if we light a match and fling it onto the petrol that insubstantial, meretricious beauty will disappear in a flash and a moment, revealing the luminous depths of the ocean. Coming to an understanding of the world is like throwing that match and comprehending the true nature of water. Be Mindful.
    Peace to All Beings,
    Your friend, Boddhipal Bhikkhu.

*   *   *

The wind had been steadily increasing in strength as I read but now it became obvious that the cyclone had arrived. There was a tremendous roar. The shutters banged and palm trees shrieked, straining against the force of the elements. It sounded as though we were in the middle of a storm at sea and I worried that a tidal wave as well as a cyclone was sweeping the city. A puddle spread out from the windows where rain was forced past the hinges. The lights blinked and then went out. I lay in the dark but it was impossible to sleep or even think. It was as though all the *bhut* in the world had gathered in a spinning circle around the city and were indulging their most destructive whims. Something in the kitchen fell and shattered on the stone floor with a report which made me sit up with a start.

    I struggled out of the mosquito-net and fumbled for some matches. The first one flared and died. The second lit but flickered uncertainly in the gusts of wind which blew under the doors, making my mosquito-net flap like a ghostly sail. I lit a hurricane lamp and went into the main room. Heavy curtains swung in front of closed windows and shutters, and the fans spun of their own volition. I wanted to be with Shiuli, to feel close to her warmth and her voice, to say anything, nothing, but hesitated. Her anger had been so sudden, so unexpected and intense. *Then don't do it near me.* I tried to explain it to myself: my insensitivity, the strain of the past few days, the discovery that Jo had been murdered. Before I could knock the bolts were drawn and her doors opened.

She looked bedraggled, as though she'd been out in the storm. Her ruby nose-stud, another new departure, flashed like a distant port light. She'd found it, along with a pair of gold cuff-links, among Jo's things and had had her nose pierced the next day, to Shomela's approval. I felt it was a little barbaric.

'I saw the light under the door,' she said.

'Can I come in?'

'Yes. You hurt me so much. I don't mean physically, though that as well. You're all I have left and you seemed to be drifting away. I'm sorry I shouted at you but I felt as though the last eighteen months had been a sham, that you felt nothing for me. I'm scared.'

'So am I. I'd be no good to you here, Shiuli. I'm fed up with the University and I'd just get more scared. I'd worry every time you left the house or every time you were ten minutes late. I think I should go, even if you don't come with me, even if I don't really want to.'

She said nothing and for a moment, before I continued, my eye was caught by the gleaming heap of discarded bangles on the table beside her bed.

'Boddhipal's letter has given me an idea. I'll go to Nepal to study and meditate, to try and get beyond all this; this flotsam of violence, cruelty and hate.'

'And love?'

I ran my fingers through her short hair. 'Perhaps even love. Shiuli, how did this work get to be so important to you?'

'It just is. If you let people die you're as bad as the murderers.'

There was a crack and a crash from the garden—one of the top-heavy palms coming down. We clung to each other, frightened by the noise.

'You can't help but let people die here, walk past them on the street. It's what that does to you which worries me. You lose your ability to feel. You kill off your emotions little by little because it's the only way to survive,' I said.

'Boddhipal would say that the suffering of one is the suffering of all, that no Buddhist can be happy while others suffer.'

'It's not happiness I'm looking for, just peace of mind and quiet. I don't think I'll be able to find it here.'

I still believed that she'd be able to convince me to stay, or that she'd change her mind and come with me. Anywhere.

* * *

We didn't hear the news until late the next morning and then had to go and confirm it with our own eyes, wishing afterwards that we hadn't. To look at a burnt-out building where you have known and loved a person, where you have spent many hours, is in some ways worse than seeing the corpse of a friend. Buildings provide the frames within which we construct our friendships.

There was the concrete shell, the cicatrice of flame and smoke arching up the walls, the gaping windows and doors. There was what remained of the simple room; a tangle of fallen concrete and twisted reinforcing rods. It was so at odds with the bright sunny day that it looked as though it must have happened a long time ago. Only the palms, their fronds hanging straight down, shrivelled and scorched, showed that the flames had leapt and jumped in the wind of the previous night.

Nazmah had telephoned. 'Is Shiuli there? How is she?'
'Not too bad.'
The line snapped and crackled at us ill-naturedly.
'I have more bad news, I'm afraid. My driver drove past Boddhipal's place this morning and says that it's totally destroyed. It was burnt down last night.'

'*Zindabad! ... Burn them!*' flared like a torch in my memory.

'Hello? Charles? Are you still there?'

'Yes.'

'He stopped to ask what had happened. The police were taking bodies out in sacks. It was set alight with petrol bombs in revenge for the Bengali settlers killed by the Shanti Bahini the day before yesterday, or whenever it was.'

'Boddhipal?' I whispered, hardly daring to listen to the answer.

'No names. My driver was told that they'd found seven bodies, all badly charred, six children and one adult. No one knew what had happened to the rest of them. Soon after it was set alight the cyclone began and the mob ran for shelter. I phoned the hospital. It's almost impossible to get any information, they're so busy dealing with people injured by the cyclone but I think I've established that no tribals have been admitted with burns. Perhaps he escaped.'

'Perhaps, yes.'

The sky was clear blue and the air still, but there were signs of the cyclone's destructive path everywhere. Cars overturned, trees uprooted and flung contemptuously aside, scraps of corrugated iron and masonry lying all over the roads. People wandered aimlessly about in the dereliction of flattened *bustees,* lifting pieces of wood and tin, peering beneath and letting them fall again. Five hundred people killed outright, the radio had estimated, but they didn't count the coastal villages or *bustees.*

There was a small group of men near the ruins of the school and Shiuli asked them what had happened to the survivors.

'They've run away, back to where they belong—the jungle,' one said, smiling.

An old man interrupted him with an impatient gesture. 'They were good people. I live near here and talked to them sometimes. They never hurt anyone. There was no reason to do this. We should be able to live in peace.' He wore a Moslem skull-cap and had the dyed beard of a Hajji, one who has made the pilgrimage to Mecca. 'The people who do things like this do them out of ignorance. They are like a man who cuts down a tree for firewood, not thinking that it shades his vegetables from the sun.'

'Do you know where they went? The ones who survived.'

'Perhaps to Nandankanan Buddhist Monastery.'

Shocked by what we'd seen and praying that Boddhipal had survived, we caught a rickshaw to the monastery. The journey took fifteen minutes but neither of us said a word, only too aware that Boddhipal would have risked his life to save the children.

* * *

Two days later I was on my way to Kathmandu, leaving behind my books and a letter of resignation to the University, but taking with me a wound which I thought immersion in the asceticism of Buddhist philosophy would heal.

Kamrul too was on the move for he had saved nearly enough money to get to Saudi Arabia and I gave him the remainder, a few thousand *taka*, as a parting gift. He wrote me a flowery letter of thanks in English, which began, 'Most honoured sir ...' and made me fear that he'd employed an official letter writer to advise him. Shomela was a more difficult proposition but I eventually decided to give her a similar amount of money and a leather-bound edition of the Koran, which seemed to please her.

Shiuli came with me to the airport. The baby-taxi was driven with even more than usual recklessness.

'Brother,' I said as we lurched from under the wheels of an oncoming truck, 'I don't want to die today.'

He laughed cheerfully and replied that such things were in the hands of Allah, not men. In truth I didn't care; death could hardly be more difficult than life and the decision to leave was a negative one. I was seeking asylum.

'Say goodbye to Nazmah for me,' I said as the little plane, a speck on the horizon, turned in from the sea and made its approach.

'I hope you find what you're looking for.'

'And you. Be careful.'

We embraced and a small crowd gathered, staring curiously at the unexpected sight.

'It's better than *Siddhartha*,' someone said.

'She's a Christian and they're married. One of his family is ill and he has to go home,' an instant myth-maker told everyone with much confidence....

I crossed the tarmac in the company of a few businessmen on their way to Calcutta, briefcases in hand, and found a seat in the cramped interior. The plane taxied out, a jeep in front to drive cows from the runway, and took off. As we turned over the tiny airport I looked down and saw Shiuli standing in a ring of still curious men. She raised her left arm, to wave or to shield her eyes from the sun and silver sparked alive on her wrist.

The suited man beside me tried to strike up a conversation but soon gave up. I went to the lavatory at the back of the plane, locked the door and sobbed like a child, ignoring the banging on the door until a sign began to blink, 'Return to your seat. Fasten your seat-belt.'

17

THE SNOW PEAKS, jagged steel against the cold sky, flushed the pink of flamingos as the sun rose away in the east, beyond Kanchenjunga and Darjeeling. The golden spire of Boddhnath Stupa flashed an answer back through the myriad prayer flags proclaiming the indivisibility of all things, animate and inanimate.

The bell hanging at the entrance to the Tara Temple, next to the Stupa, rang twice; the first supplicants of the day. Carrying brass dishes containing offerings of jasmine and rice they sprinkled a little at the feet of the Buddha, made some devotional gestures and left. I never tired of watching devotees express their belief in this way; it seemed as natural to them as eating and sleeping.

Downstairs Yangchenla, my landlord's daughter, came to milk the cow; I heard her talking to herself or to the cow as she clanked the bucket into place.

The activity around the Stupa, the everyday waking of the village, imposed itself on the mirage of Chittagong; I'd been back there, back in Shiuli's city, with her, with her voice and touch and love. I was exhausted but the storm had abated; the night's horrors and humiliations had blown through and out of my mind as though the memories belonged to someone else, an acquaintance.

Living at Boddhnath it was not possible to be immune to the power of the mountains. They changed from day to day and season to season with a calm purposefulness, irrespective of humanity. At times they appeared bright and friendly, at others, when the clouds clung around the topmost rocks or streamed away in an icy wind, they were as mysterious and all-knowing as the Buddha Sakyamuni himself. Sometimes they were dark and threatening, ready to destroy anyone with the temerity to approach. I once said as much to Lama Govinda but he thought the concept foolish.

'It is us who change, not the mountains. We impose our

prejudices and ideas onto what we observe, imagining that we have an identity separate from that which we experience.'

Escaping Chittagong had been a surrender to a concept of dualism which had been denied and resolved by the Buddha. I had tried to use Buddhism as a method of retreat, as a way of destroying my need for Shiuli, but it transformed me. I realised that my love for her and the complementary fear which her work inspired in me were to be embraced as one; conflict is as inevitable as death. Shiuli learnt that there is nothing to fear but fear a long time ago.

I had surrendered the afternoon we went to see the wreckage of Boddhipal's school, where we were scorched by despair as surely as were the palms by fire—there seemed to be no end to disaster—and as the rickshaw carried us away from the intolerable sight, through the crowded streets towards Nandankanan monastery, I knew that whether Boddhipal was alive or dead I had to leave; I could no longer pretend that I could support a fear which had rooted itself too deeply to be dislodged. Nor, I knew and accepted for the first time, would I be able to persuade Shiuli into accompanying me to any refuge.

The rickshaw carried us under the monastery's ugly, Asokan-style, concrete gateway and through a small garden bright with the pinks and reds of hibiscus flowers. The driver executed a faultless U-turn and stopped with a proud smile in front of the open hallway.

The monks were eating their midday meal, the last of the day, sitting cross-legged in a circle with their plates of rice and vegetables on the floor in front of them. We waited on a bench outside the refectory while the head of the monastery finished eating.

He was a plump, contented-looking Bengali, and he made us follow him to his room where he washed, settled himself into a chair and called for tea before he would listen to a word. The room was little bigger than Boddhipal's had been, and equally bare and ascetic.

He expressed dismay when Shiuli told him that Boddhipal's monastery and school had been burnt down the previous night and my heart sank—he obviously hadn't seen or heard anything of those who had escaped.

'We think it may have been done in retaliation for the murder of Bengali settlers in the Hill Tracts the other day.'

'Ah yes, very probable. Terrible thing.'

Three cups of tea were brought by a boy monk and our host relapsed into silence, drumming his fingers lightly on his stomach, as though recalling the meal he'd just finished. Shiuli and I sat hopelessly beside each other, neither knowing what to do next nor feeling strong enough for whatever it might be. Rousing himself he addressed us, 'You must come and see our hair relic of the Buddha. Yes, yes, no question but you must.'

He led us down an open corridor and into the temple which was dark and smelt strongly of incense. At one end a white-painted Buddha wearing orange robes stood out ghostlike above offerings of flowers.

He unlocked a door with a key which hung on a string round his neck and we followed him into a small room with a barred window set high in one wall. There was nothing inside save a table on which lay a lacquered Burmese box, intricately decorated with gold and red dragons. It was unlocked and from within the folds of a velvet cloth he drew forth a thin crystal phial, discoloured with age, which he held carefully up to the light. Inside there were a few strands of fine black hair and I tried to tell myself that it was important, that I was privileged to be looking at a relic of the Gautama, the All-Enlightened One, born more than two thousand five hundred years ago. It didn't work, I could only wonder what He would have thought of the desire to preserve parts of his body, and remember that he was supposed to have been cremated. I recalled the words of the dying Buddha to his disciple Ananda, words which Boddhipal had often repeated:

'Be your own island, be your own refuge. Do not take any other refuge. Let the Teaching be your island, let the Teaching be your refuge; do not take any other refuge.'

Shiuli looked glassily at the phial. She seemed dazed and I realised she'd been living on her nerves for days; it was beginning to show.

'In 1958 we presented part of this holy relic to Sri Lanka and another part to Japan six years later. It is our greatest treasure.'

He replaced the phial in the box and re-locked it. 'We shall try to find out what has happened to Boddhipal Bhikkhu and to the others but if they have returned to their villages it will be difficult to discover which of them have survived.'

He covered a yawn as we went back through the shrine and then, seeming to notice Shiuli's misery for the first time, he smiled at her. 'Remember the story of the grain of mustard seed. A mother came weeping and wailing to the All-Compassionate One carrying the corpse of her baby in her arms and begged Him to restore the child to life.

'Lord Buddha listened carefully and then asked her to bring him a single grain of mustard seed from a household in which no one had died. The woman searched all day and night but couldn't find a house in which no one had died. She returned to the Buddha the next day and admitted her failure.

'"You see," He said, "there is no one in the world who has not suffered what you suffer. The world shares your grief; it is in the nature of this physical space we inhabit."'

He put his soft hands together and with more apologies for not being able to help, muttered, '*Namushkar.*'

We were left feeling as though we'd attempted some simple task and failed. The parable hardly helped, for it was familiar and Boddhipal had told it more convincingly.

'We could try the police and the fire station,' I suggested without enthusiasm as we walked through the garden and out under the gateway.

'We'd be wasting our time and come away more depressed than we are now.'

'Journalists?'

'It's an idea but I think that if Boddhipal's alive he'll contact us sooner or later. He'll know we're worried.'

She beckoned a passing rickshaw driver but he didn't notice so I shouted at him, 'Hey! Empty one! Here!'

The driver was old and he coughed consumptively as he

turned the battered machine towards us, straining against the pedals. In the recesses of my mind I heard an echo: *Change is necessary in a society in which most people are permanently malnourished.*

I told Shiuli I'd see her later and called another rickshaw driver, searching feverishly through my wallet for Abu Zafar Hashim's card at the same time. I felt confident that he'd be able to help and it was with a sense of elation that I asked the driver to take me to Andher Killa, to the newspaper office. He made an infinitesimal gesture with his head; the rickshaw driver's grudging assent, as though to say, 'I'd rather not but I have no choice.'

* * *

Hashim had a journalist's memory and greeted me by name when I was ushered into his office by a peon, although it was eighteen months since we'd met briefly on the ferry to Cox Bazar.

His office, more like a cubicle off the press room, was cramped and made more so by the piles of badly stacked back issues and files. On his desk was a copy of *China Reconstructs* and an ancient Remington typewriter.

'Did you enjoy your holiday in Cox Bazar?' he asked without interest, shaking my hand and sweeping a pile of newspaper cuttings off a chair.

'I did, yes. I hope I'm not disturbing you.'

'No, no, not at all.'

I could see that I was.

He pushed the typewriter to one side and tossed the magazine into a dusty corner. 'It's as full of lies as *Time,* but it's better than nothing.'

As he sat down opposite me I noticed that a yellowish smallpox scar obliterated the pupil of one eye; it was sightless.

'I went into the Hill Tracts from Cox Bazar.'

He raised his eyebrows a fraction. 'Did you? How interesting.' He sounded cautious but his good eye didn't waver.

'But I didn't come about that.'

He relaxed a little but kept looking at me. 'Not a social visit then? Ahmed! Tea!'

I wasn't sure how to approach the subject. I'd been convinced that he'd be willing to help but now, faced with him, I realised that I knew nothing of his beliefs or prejudices. I plunged in, throwing caution to the winds. 'Last night a mob burnt down a monastery and school run by a group of tribal monks.'

'I know.' It wasn't an encouragement to continue.

'One of the monks was a friend of mine.'

'Which one?'

I was immediately suspicious. 'Does it matter?'

'Forgive me. A journalist's curiosity.'

I hesitated. I'd been going to ask him if he knew where the survivors were but realised that he had no reason to trust me. A *nation of conspirators,* Shiuli had said; conspirators suspect everyone else of conspiring too. I could belong to any one of numerous political groupings, national or international, as far as he knew.

'Are you going to print the story?'

He was saved from an immediate response by the arrival of tea, but once Ahmed had left he said, 'All my journalists are working on the cyclone, and the political situation of course. Why do you ask?'

'Because I think it's important—'

'Do you have any information?'

'Not really. Seven dead, one adult and six children. All unidentifiable. The rest have disappeared, not at the hospital, not at Nandankanan monastery.'

'Do you know where they are?'

'I hoped you'd be able to tell me.'

'I'm afraid not.'

I had the impression he was holding something back, perhaps only because I'd been expecting to ask the questions, not be questioned. It was an impasse and we were both silent; he obviously wasn't going to say anything else. Suddenly I was angry and I didn't care how many enemies I made in the last few days; the decision to leave had been taken, it was irrevocable.

'I suppose they're only tribals, only uncultured savages or unreasoning guerrillas to you. It doesn't matter how many die. In fact the more the merrier.'

He put his empty tea cup neatly in the centre of the saucer. 'It's not that. Ahmed! Tea! Five hundred killed by the cyclone they say, although fifteen hundred would be nearer the mark, if you count the *bustees,* the coastal villages and the fishermen who never heard the warning—'

'So seven more doesn't count? Not a slow news day? They're only tribals, after all.'

'You don't understand—'

'Or do I understand too well?' I stood up.

'Sit down, sit down please. Let me explain how it is to be publishing a newspaper under martial law.'

'Go on.'

'Thank you.' He drew a square on a blank sheet of paper and squinted critically at the result with his undamaged eye. 'At the moment the most we could print would be a factual account. You know the kind of thing, a paragraph giving the barest bones of the event. But that is not satisfying or even interesting. There should be something on the follow-up. Who are the suspects? Why was it done? What are the police doing? Interviews with the survivors. Are you with me?'

'Yes. What are the police doing?'

He pushed a lock of curly hair back from his scarred forehead and waited in silence for Ahmed to put down more tea and close the door again. 'They are doing the same as us. Nothing. Yet they too have their suspects and know why it was done. The fact is, my friend, that we cannot run the story without being closed down.'

'I'm not with you. Why?'

He drew a circle and then dropped the pen with a sigh, fed up with either the design or the conversation. He spoke quickly. 'The army is in power. The army has a political front, it is called the People's Party, and the army is fighting in the Chittagong Hill Tracts.' He stopped and looked at me as though he'd explained everything.

I was more confused than ever. 'It was the army?'

'Not exactly, you don't quite understand.' He sounded exasperated and continued as though he were speaking to a child. 'Every political party in Bangladesh has its paid thugs, its *goondars*. Yes?'

I nodded dumbly.

'We cannot write up the story because the leaders of last night's attack on your friend's monastery were two well-known People's Party *goondars*. If we suggest, however discreetly, that the military's pet party was involved then we'll receive the same treatment ourselves. It's best to leave it alone for the moment.'

'For the moment?'

'The situation will change tomorrow, next month, next year. Sometime the government will change. We talked about this before.'

'It'll be a bit late by then.'

He shrugged. 'What do you expect me to do? I cannot leave Bangladesh, and going underground is not a sensible option, for me.'

* * *

As the fruit bats returned from the south, flying like laden sailing ships, it was the irredeemable seconds of tenderness with Shiuli which came back to me; the kisses and glances, the soft hilarity of lovemaking, the shiver of her crippled leg and the times we lay still in the heat just touching fingers. I thought of the long build-up to the monsoon and the *krishnachura* trees trailing their scarlet flowers like cascades of blood over Chittagong's gardens and streets, over the tired residue of Pandita Vihara, its bricks reverting to the centuries-old alluvium from which they were baked.

Yangchenla came up to exchange half a pint of milk for an English lesson before taking the cow out to graze. I'd learnt no Tibetan and our conversations were, of necessity, in stilted Nepali laced with a few English words. But her mind was never on English and I only managed to impart a few phrases useful in dealing with tourists. She stood there looking at me, waiting for me to address her. I saw a young Tibetan. She could have been no other race with her wide, candid face, ruddy cheeks and slanted eyes always on the edge of a smile or a laugh, a half-woman, half-girl to whom I represented something foreign and incalculable. Did she see anything of the failure of the spirit which made me leave Chittagong, or of the determination to return? I had no doubt that it was what I had to do. I had been wasting my time in Kathmandu. Shiuli was the only important thing in my life.

'I will leave, even before the swallows migrate south,' I told Yangchenla. 'Perhaps this week.'

She said nothing.

'It's been eighteen months and there are things I must do,' I added lamely. 'I left my ... my wife in Chittagong, where I taught before I came here, and I must return to her now.'

Yangchenla was suddenly interested and came into the room, smiling as she prepared to question me about this previously unheard-of 'wife'.

The caterpillar buries itself in the high pastureland of the Himalayas to try, unsuccessfully, to rid itself of *Cordyceps Senensis* burning into its nervous system. I'd imagined that its development was arrested there, at the second instar, but I was wrong; the metamorphosis occurs but in a new direction. Instead of creating a cocoon which hardens into the protective shell of a pupa and then developing the wings, the perfect form, the colours of *Papilio Krishna Krishna,* the caterpillar is transformed into the fungus which pushes its crude brown stalk an inch above the surface of the thin soil.

18

THE AIR-HOSTESS brought orange juice as the plane banked over Calcutta and the Hooghly Bridge, that mass of confused steel spanning the river like a switch-back. It dropped behind us into its own haze of pollution and our shadow skated across the broken, dry land, across fields and villages, rivers and canals, across Bengal. We turned south, out over the Bay and down the coast, where the millennial feud between land and sea continues, neither side winning. Gusts of wind ruffled the surface of the water where the Mouths of the Ganga mix with and muddy the sea surrounding thousands of tiny islets. I day-dreamed and watched the hard glitter off the ocean. It was right to return now, to face the reality of conflict and not be afraid, confident in the knowledge acquired in study. I held off the happiness, teasing myself with anticipation, like a juggler with bottles, not allowing them to be still, defying gravity's power to draw them down and shatter them.

The familiar city, balanced between river and sea, its hills greener than I remembered, came into view. Chittagong: which Ibn Batuta, in 1346, called 'a great place situated on the shore of the great sea'. I glimpsed the onion-shaped tower of the Armenian church; trees and bushes enveloped the graveyard and crept up over the sides of the church, blurring its edges.

My skin goosefleshed and tears of sentimentality pricked my eyelids as I thought of Shiuli. It seemed extraordinary that I'd managed to stay away so long, even absurd that I'd left in the first place, succumbing to my fears like a child to nightmares. On the horizon lay a ragged disarray of white clouds, whipped up like froth on the shining sea.

To my surprise I breezed through Immigration; they hardly glanced at my passport and accepted easily that I was on holiday. I joked with the Customs officers in Bengali and, flattered that I treated them as equals, they waved me through indulgently. Contrary to expectations everything had gone well; I'd had no trouble getting a visa from the Bangladesh Embassy in Kathmandu, the flights had been underbooked and the weather fine. I felt that I was stepping back into a past I knew well, and one which called me through layers of time, like a residual race memory, or a myth.

Leaving the air-conditioned airport building and walking into the sunlight had none of the shock it has during the thick, oppressive summer months, and as my eyes adjusted to the glare it was as though I'd never left Chittagong, as though my memory had played me false, painting a bleaker picture of the city and of its inhabitants than they deserved. Even the baby-taxi drivers were less aggressive than I remembered.

'Armenitola.' The word rolled off my tongue pleasurably. I savoured and repeated it. 'Armenitola. Number 1, Armenian Street. Thirty-five *taka*.'

'Yes sahib.'

No more discussion or argument was necessary and I laughed at the simplicity of it. I laughed again at the problem the driver had starting the engine. Once it was going we puttered off, past Patenga with its black coal boats and up the dock road; cranes, crates, containers, incongruous amongst the palm trees, and the ships themselves, rusty hulks for the most part, trading under obscure flags of convenience, apart from a grey French frigate riding at anchor in the centre of the river (there must be champagne somewhere in the city, I thought briefly). On the other side, in the paddy fields, the winter rice showed half an inch above the surface of the water, and the sunlight which slanted across the land lit up each blade individually, making them glow like green fire. Never had Bangladesh appeared so peaceful or alluring. A square-rigged cargo boat beat upstream. 'Wheat. A gift of the European Economic Community' was printed in block letters on a sack which had been used to patch the sail billowing out from its crooked mast. On the built-up stern, high above the water-line, a man was silhouetted against the sky. He held the tiller of a heavy, leaf-shaped rudder in both hands, looking for all the world as though he and the boat had been plucked from an Egyptian hieroglyph and set down in Bengal's delta system. Near the far bank a fisherman, balanced on a butterfly-like bamboo structure, swung his net out of the water. A long reed-shaped boat rocked below him as he bounced his hand on the glistening mesh to bring a few fish flapping in the taut net within reach.

The driver chatted above the clatter of his engine and didn't insist when I told him I didn't have any dollars to change and didn't want a girl.

'You live in Armenian Street don't you?' he asked.

'I used to.'

'Yes, I remember. That old foreigner, does he still live there?'

'He died.'

'A year ago my brother's child died—he spent three thousand *taka* on doctors' bills and hospitals, all to no purpose....' His family history poured out easily and fluently. I was pleased to find that I could understand all he said, but the streets demanded my attention and after a few minutes I was in the grip of my senses, gorged on noises, smells, colours and the hot, dry air. What had Shiuli said the first time we met? 'Here, your senses tell you you're alive all the time, whether the experience is pleasant or not.'

Tiger Pass, Station Road, the Ujala Cinema and New Market, past the Armoury and into Alkaran Road, where I asked the driver to stop. I bought half a dozen jasmine garlands and some milk sweets: dark brown *kalojam* and some *roshigulo*, Shiuli's favourite. I looped the flowers over one hand and clung on with the other as the driver negotiated pot-holes and pedestrians at speed. The scent of the star-shaped flowers invaded the air like a thin mist.

The streets narrowed and the traffic became more dense, the city's open spaces and palm-covered hills replaced by confused crowds of colour. Thick shadows chopped the twisting lanes.

'Red monkey! Red monkey!' a child shouted, running alongside the baby-taxi and grinning in at me. It seemed unmalicious and I was surprised, remembering how often the repeated phrase had once angered me.

'Black monkey!' I said as he dropped behind, making his grin broaden.

*   *   *

I pushed on the towering street doors and then again, harder. They opened reluctantly, with a grinding noise, and stuck fast. I squeezed through the gap and found myself face to face with the ragged disorganisation of a slum shelter. An old woman crouching before a pitiful fire of green wood gazed at me suspiciously. Two tiny children sorted deftly through a pile of rubbish stacked up next to her shelter.

'It's private here,' she said. It was a statement of fact rather than a claim to ownership.

'I know.'

She went back to her task without further comment. Skirting her hovel I made my way towards the house, noticing that she or her family had cut down many bushes and small trees for firewood. The herringbone brick path was overgrown with tall weeds and it was only as I pushed through them that I felt the first detonations of disquiet, damped down by the realisation that Kamrul had left at the same time as myself. Perhaps there had been no gardener since then, for over a year. How he would have hated to see it overgrown and untidy.

The green Venetian shutters were closed, as they often had been in summer but rarely in winter, and I mounted the wide veranda steps with foreboding. At the top I stopped, shocked by the desolation. Dust, peeled whitewash and fallen plaster covered the tiles, but it was the plants which took my breath away. The red-clay pots were still there, hanging from the walls and suspended between the high arches overlooking the garden. Only the blood thorn showed any sign of life, its dangerous spikes protecting two or three tiny leaves. The rest, the gardenia, the delicate ferns and lilies were withered and dry, as though poisoned.

A gecko moved above the main door, making me jump, and a few flakes of whitewash fluttered down to join the undisturbed line of white dust lying at the foot of the wall.

I crossed the veranda quickly and pushing my fingers through the shutter slats, I pulled. The shutters gave an inch; a heavy chain was wrapped through and around them, fastened in front with an old-fashioned, iron padlock. The noise disturbed a few crows in their palm fastnesses and they cawed ill-naturedly. Between the slats I could feel that the glass interior doors were also closed. Peering in I dimly made out the tall, glassed-in bookshelves, the shadowy portrait of Vazken of Echmiadzin, Supreme Catholicos of all Armenians, and the heavy Empire furniture, but no sign of life. The house could have been empty and unlived in for twenty or even sixty years, awaiting the inevitable roof collapse and the wrecking power of a single summer's rain.

I dropped my bag and the box of sweets and forced up the shutters of Shiuli's room; everything was neat and tidy, as a room might be left before a long trip abroad. The cupboards were closed, the desk clear and the mosquito net looped up above her bed. Dust lay over everything, even caught in the dry strands on the other side of the glass where a spider's transparent skeleton hung isolated in the centre of its web. I tapped on the glass and may even have shouted 'Shiuli!' but the only response was the angry mocking of the crows. I ran the length of the veranda, dust puffing dully up over my sandals, to the shutters of what had been my room. My books were as I'd left them and Nataraj stood in the same futile pose. Without looking further I slammed down the slats.

The back of the house was also shuttered and locked, closed off with a finality which seemed to deny the immediate past, as though Shiuli and I had never belonged there in the first place. My mind raced, rejecting the thought which engulfed it as though one cell wall after another had burst, leaving the greyest and most dismal sludge of conclusions.

The rubbish picker had followed me to the back of the house and her voice grated on my nerves. 'Who do you want?'

'Shiuli,' I said, more to myself than to the old hag.

'Who? She's inside.'

I tried to force open the rusty garden tap to get a drink

and the woman scratched at my arm with a hand as dry and bony as the claw of a bird. 'Please give me some money.' Shaking her off I thrust my hand into a pocket and withdrew a handful of Nepalese, Indian and Bangladeshi *paise* which, in my hurry, I gave her carelessly. They scattered across the dusty ground. The jasmine garlands broke from my wrist and lay in the dust like useless, broken porcelain. She knelt to pick up the coins, one by one.

I shouted at the top of my voice, 'Shiuli!' and sat down suddenly on the steps, my legs giving way beneath me. Three crows hopped off a branch in the mango tree and flopped down to check on what the old woman was gathering with such patience.

Two slats in the shutter above my head snapped open and Shomela's red-rimmed old eyes stared out at me, blinking in the light. 'Go away!'

'Shomela! It's me, Charles. Don't you recognise me? Shomela, what's happened? Where's Shiuli?'

'Go away!'

'What do you mean? It's Charles...'

'I know who it is. Go away.'

'Shomela... What happened?'

Her voice rose. 'Go away, don't come back.'

'Where's Shiuli? I won't go until you tell me where she is.'

The slats snapped shut again.

The old rubbish picker squatted on her haunches in the shade of the mango tree to watch, no emotion showing on her narrow face.

I hammered on the doors with both fists and shouted at Shomela to come back. I spoke quietly, I made impossible promises and finally, like a child, threatened to break the door down. My hands were black with dust and the knuckles grazed where I'd forced them through the shutters to try and reach the bolts inside.

After twenty minutes I was dizzy from dehydration and lack of food—I hadn't eaten since breakfast in Calcutta—so picking up my bag (the box of sweets had been taken—by the old woman's half-starved children no doubt) I pushed my way back through the undergrowth and out onto the busy street.

I bought a cheap, badly-made axe and ordered a meal in a restaurant, not tasting the hot food.

By the time I emerged the street was preparing itself for the fast approaching night; rickshaw drivers hung hurricane lamps beneath their machines, the chant from the mosques rose slowly into the cool air and a woman, tightly concealed in a *burkha*, slipped hurriedly through a doorway. The noisy, shifting mass of rickshaws and men, smelling of work, swayed and moved like dreamers.

Parked beside the high compound wall, above which only the tallest palms showed, was Nazmah's black Mercedes; no one else in the city had such an ancient or immaculate vehicle. It gleamed in the half-darkness, amongst the street's detritus, like something from another world. Her driver slept inside, with his head on his chest.

The old woman was feeding her reluctant fire inside the gateway and the green wood crackled and spat. Her children huddled together nearby, a piece of dirty jute sacking clasped around their shoulders.

The main veranda doors were open, and laying the axe against the outside wall I took a deep breath and stepped back into the high, dark room. A yellow light shone through the half-open door of what had been Jo's room and I heard women's voices. Plaster and dust crunched beneath my shoes and as I made my way towards the light I knocked into a chair.

Nazmah appeared in the doorway. 'Who's there? Who is it?' she demanded, her voice echoing strangely. The light fell on my face and she recognised me. 'Charles....'

'Yes. Where's Shiuli? What happened here, Nazmah? Shomela wouldn't tell me anything. She wouldn't even speak to me.'

'She blames you.'

'What for? What did I do?'

'You left....'

'And Shiuli?'

'She's gone too, Charles. I'll tell you about it later.' Her tone was businesslike, almost unfriendly. 'I'm just fixing something up for Shomela before I go.'

She turned back into Jo's room, leaving me with a sensation of sudden emptiness, as though eviscerated.

I blundered into Jo's dusty room and was waved impatiently to a chair by Nazmah. Shomela stared at me blankly for a moment but said nothing. They were poring over papers, held down by glass paperweights, on Jo's old desk. Nazmah seemed to be explaining something to Shomela, but I was too tired and confused to try and understand what she was saying. Restlessly getting out of the chair I peered at a few photographs without seeing them until I came across a portrait of Jo and Shiuli together. He, a paunchy fifty-year-old in a white bush shirt, ill at ease in the unfamiliar surroundings of a photographer's studio, and she, a slight teenager staring boldly into the camera. The picture had been garishly hand-coloured and Shiuli's skin so lightened that she looked almost European. The painted backdrop depicted a lake, fountains and formal, Mughal gardens—the famed Shalimar perhaps. They were far from the two people I had known, even their stances were unfamiliar.

I turned on Nazmah angrily. 'You must tell me. Where is she? I've a right to know.'

'No Charles, you have no rights. I will tell you but you must wait. You won't be able to see her.'

She returned to the papers and I paced the veranda as impatiently as a caged animal waiting to be fed.

'Sorry I was so long,' Nazmah said when she finally emerged from Jo's room. 'Shiuli asked me to arrange Shomela's retirement. There are a few legal things to sort out.'

'Where's Shiuli?'

'Shomela's bitter because she regarded Shiuli as her daughter, and dutiful daughters are supposed to stay at home to look after their parents in old age.'

'Where is she, Nazmah?'

'She's gone, joined the Shanti Bahini. Bloody fool.' Nazmah

put the full force of her arrogance into the phrase. 'Come on.'

'Where to?'

'Home. You can't stay here.'

I stumbled after Nazmah's thin figure, through the overgrown garden and past the old woman's slum hut, to the Mercedes. Nazmah settled herself languorously into the back of the car, arranging her sari around her and loosening her fine Kashmir shawl, the kind that will pass through a woman's ring as easily as smoke.

'A few months after you left Shiuli was arrested. When I found out I got my father onto it immediately. He telephoned around a little and soon discovered that she was being held by the army, so it was more serious and delicate than if it had been some stupid police officer. You'd have thought that with my father's connections he could have done something, but no.... I've got nothing to say to her now, you know that, Charles? It's strange to see her—'

'So she got out eventually?'

'Yes—'

The car screeched to a halt and the driver swore quietly at a rickshaw, with no hurricane lamp hanging below, which had shot out from a side turning. He re-started the engine and we moved off smoothly and softly, sliding round obstructions and over pot-holes.

'She got out after three months of pretty constant pressure. My father was so frustrated that he finally spoke to our beloved President. That did the trick, but he had to give his word that Shiuli would behave.'

'What was it about? What had she done?'

'Didn't you get my letter? I wrote before the arrest saying that she was in trouble and that you should come back.'

'I never got it.'

'She'd been compiling a dossier of atrocities, rapes, murders, etcetera by the army in the Hill Tracts—she was planning to take it to the United Nations Human Rights Committee. It would have been a little embarrassing, nothing more, for the government and for the aid donors. It was nothing.'

'But how was she?'

'Terrible, Charles; she'd been raped and tortured. All her old softness had been beaten out of her. She talked only about Ila Mitra.'

'Who's Ila Mitra?'

'Don't you know?'

We turned in at the gates of Nazmah's father's house and the guard saluted as the driver changed into first for the steep drive. I stared gloomily at the modern white façade, wondering how I would manage to get through an evening of Mushtaque pontificating drunkenly. But Nazmah told me that her parents were in Brunei for a few days.

We sat on rugs in a vast, tiled room, before a fire of teak logs. A servant appeared with two glasses of whisky and a jug of iced water.

'Bring the bottle and then you can go, Saleem,' Nazmah said. She waited for him to return and leave the bottle before continuing. 'Shiuli was ill and bitter; it was only her anger which kept her alive at first. She talked at me when I went to see her, spitting out her hatred of the army, not caring whether I was interested or not. When she was tired of the subject, or tired of herself, she talked about Ila Mitra.'

'You said. Who is she?'

'She's an old woman now, living in Calcutta, but she was a heroine in 1949. Ila Mitra,' I recognised Nazmah's lecturing voice, when she delved back into her remarkable memory and talked without apparent thought or pause, as though the words were there already, just waiting for the tap to be opened, 'Ila Mitra came from a family of Hindu landowners and had married into the same class, a landlord in Rajshahi in the north. She was thirty in 1949 and a member of the Communist Party. In that year she helped to organise forty-five thousand tribal and Moslem sharecroppers to demand a reasonable percentage of the rice grown with their sweat. They wanted a third. The landlords didn't like the movement and sent in their *goondars*, then the police. The peasants had two shotguns and bows and arrows, that was all. They fought off the police twice, then the army was called in, and that was the end. Ila Mitra was framed and charged with murder. In jail she was horrifically tortured and during the trial made a statement to the court in which she told the whole story, from beginning to end, in detail. It was the first time that a woman had stood up in a court and described the kind of torture used on her; things which no one should ever have to say. It was no good, of course, the forces against her were too powerful and she was sentenced to transportation for life under Section 302 of the Penal Code. Four years later the Moslem League lost the election and finally, in 1956, Ila Mitra was released.'

We watched the fire blazing in the grate. A great log burnt through and broke, sending a cloud of angry sparks flaring up the chimney.

'Shiuli didn't tell me what she was going to do but I could see that she was planning something. I told her she was a fool to fight for a lost cause, that the tribals have no chance—'

'All causes start off by being lost.'

'Maybe you're right,' she said eventually, 'but Shiuli wanted revenge.'

'Surely not.'

'You didn't see her, Charles. Fierceness was the only thing left; she wasn't the person either of us knew. We had nothing to talk about, nothing in common.'

'Did she ever talk about me?'

'The only thing I remember her saying was, "He'll find the mountains aren't enough." One morning I went down to Armenitola and she'd gone; there was a letter which said she was going away and that it was unlikely we'd meet again. It wasn't very friendly—I felt betrayed.'

I gulped down a glassful of whisky and refilled it, almost wanting to laugh at my own stupidity for coming back; for thinking that things remain the same, and for learning nothing.

'I didn't tell you that I'm going to Paris, did I? I've been offered a post at the Maison des Sciences des Hommes. That's why I had to sort out Shomela's things today; I catch the Dhaka-Delhi flight next week. It was time to leave anyway. I advise you to do the same.'

'How do you know she's joined the Shanti Bahini?'

'I don't, Charles, but there was nowhere else for her to go if she followed her own logic.'

'I'll go and stay in Armenitola for a bit. She may come back.'

'You're mad. She'll never come back.'

'I'd like to stay there anyway, at least while ...' I'd been going to say, 'while I decide what to do next,' but there seemed little point.

'Suit yourself. I'm going to bed now. There's more whisky if you want it.'

Lying before the dying fire I finished the bottle.

* * *

Nazmah gave me a lift to Armenitola the next morning, then took Shomela to her new house. I carried Shomela's bag to the gate and when I said goodbye she held my hand in both of hers for a second. Sentimentality or forgiveness? An apology perhaps. It was the first time we had ever touched.

Nazmah came once afterwards, the day she left for Delhi and Paris. It was an embarrassing farewell, for we had little to say to each other and avoided the subject of Shiuli.

After they'd gone I went to look for the *shiuli* tree. There was no trace of it or of its strange ephemeral flowers, apart from a narrow stump, hacked and broken off a foot above the ground. Feeling a foolish compulsion to assuage the spirit of the tree I sprinkled rice and vermilion over it, then lit a clay oil lamp before it. Finally, finding a rusty saw in Kamrul's old room, I cut the torn wood off straight, and watched uncomprehendingly by a couple of children smeared pitch over its white, sappy surface.

I hope it will shoot from the roots, that the heavy, damp soil is still feeding the thousands of root filaments and a dull, unpromising node near the base is preparing itself for the sudden conversion into a bud. Winter is no time to return; there is no sensuality in dust. Was there only sensation at a pitch of sweat and desire?

I ransacked the house for a note or a letter from Shiuli, but found nothing amongst her silk saris and law books. Then I lay under a fan in one of the dark rooms, mine I suppose, smoking ganja. When it ran out I walked the few hundred yards to a government opium shop and by bribing the man I acquired enough of the sticky black drug to buy calm.

I have established a slow rhythm, avoiding all decisions and gradually eating my way through Shomela's stocks of rice, lentils and vegetables.

Some days ago another family of rubbish pickers moved into the compound and someone now keeps a dilapidated rickshaw inside the gate. One evening the radio, my only link with the outside world, was stolen. I didn't bother to question the families or call the police; there would have been little point.

I have carried a mat up onto the flat roof, and in the cool evenings I stare up through the slatted palm leaves which droop over the house, listening to the crows fighting over scraps. Once one of the rubbish pickers' children climbed sixty feet up a palm to cut down some coconuts. I watched him without emotion, as one might watch an ant; I wouldn't have moved had he fallen. They know that this is their place now.

Yesterday, or the day before, Major Rahman came, appearing suddenly on the veranda, standing, threateningly, over me. He held out a piece of flimsy, closely printed paper covered in official stamps; a deportation order. 'I don't know how you got a visa and I don't care, but you have twenty-four hours to be gone.' His nervous hand movements were less fluid than I remembered and it made him more mechanical, somehow. For the first time I saw him as just another army officer, with no distinguishing features. My mistake all along had been to imagine that he was anything other than a professional soldier, a killer.

'Sit down, Major; it's a long time since we met.' And because I was in the mood to hurt asked after his wife.

He didn't sit down but after a pause he said, 'Where's Shiuli? Did you think she'd be here waiting for you?'

For the first time I hated him and his type as I had never hated before: his good looks and well-trained manner, his Sandhurst accent and all he represented.

'I don't know where Shiuli is.'

He stared at me as though to say it wasn't necessary to dissemble. 'Don't try and follow her. The jungle isn't an hospitable place and I have men outside. She may have given them the slip but you wouldn't.'

'The British High Commissioner....'

'Agrees, unofficially, that it would be best if you left the country.' He marched out like the machine he is; click, click down the steps, and I laughed on the empty veranda.

* * *

I took a mosquito net onto the roof, set it up with some bamboo supports and crawled inside, into the protective web.

Perhaps Rahman's soldiers won't find me up here.

Through the white membrane the stars and the Milky Way fall away like a million spores released into a late spring sky. Spores which drift and die or settle on a caterpillar in the high valleys. So the wasteful, unforgiving cycle of change and renewal continues, unspoilt and uninterrupted.